HIS PREGNANT
CHRISTMAS
PRINCESS

HIS PREGNANT CHRISTMAS PRINCESS

LEAH ASHTON

MILLS & BOON

First published in Great Britain 2018
by Mills & Boon, an imprint of HarperCollins*Publishers*
1 London Bridge Street, London, SE1 9GF

Large Print edition 2019

© 2018 Leah Ashton

ISBN: 978-0-263-08225-8

MIX
Paper from
responsible sources
FSC™ C007454

This book is produced from independently certified
FSC™ paper to ensure responsible forest management. For
more information visit www.harpercollins.co.uk/green.

Printed and bound in Great Britain
by CPI Group (UK) Ltd, Croydon, CR0 4YY

For Linley.

A wonderful friend,
and a wonderful writer.

(Also, for Gidget. Just because.)

PROLOGUE

One year ago

THE VELA ADA CITY LIBRARY was usually bustling on a Wednesday afternoon. Students would be studying at the small cluster of high-sided carrel desks beyond the rows of bookshelves, or chatting in groups on the brightly coloured sofas. Toddlers would try to sit neatly cross-legged beside babies cradled on parents' laps, listening in rapt attention to stories or nursery rhymes read by one of the librarians. And, of course, library patrons of every age would dot the aisles, or borrow books at the self-serve kiosks, or come to ask questions at the information desk.

Ana Tomasich stood at that information desk now, but the library was empty and silent. In her hand she held an opened envelope made of thick, expensive paper, and she turned that envelope over and over in her hands, rubbing her thumb occasionally over the elaborately embossed broken seal.

Outside, it was already dark on the tiny Mediterranean island, with the sun setting at four p.m. this Christmas Eve. Through the large glass windows at the front of the historic sandstone library building she could see the streets, crisscrossed with Christmas lights stretching between the cast-iron lamp posts that edged the cobblestone streets of Vela Ada's modest capital city.

If she stood at a particular angle near the large print section, Ana knew she would also be able to see the huge, towering Christmas tree that stood, magnificent and twinkling, outside City Hall, only a short walk down the street. And from next to the after-hours return chute she'd have a view all the way down to the Vela Ada marina, also decked out in elaborate Christmas lights, with angels and stars glittering above the swell of the Adriatic Sea.

But for now Ana was perfectly happy to just stand in the quiet of the library, her gaze travelling aimlessly over the paper angels that hung from the ceiling—she'd helped a group of six-year-olds to make them last week—and then to the four Christmas trees of varying heights that she and the other librarians had had great fun decorating, with lights and other arts and crafts creations from the children who visited the library.

This year she'd had some of the older kids plant *pšenica*—wheat—in saucers, for the Feast of St Lucia. Tradition stated that the height of the wheat by Christmas directly correlated to the luck and prosperity you would experience the following year. The saucers had all grown tall, bushy wheat—but, although Ana couldn't really define her emotions right now, she wouldn't say she was feeling lucky.

The library had closed early today and would open again in the New Year. All the other library staff had headed home, but Ana had volunteered to lock up, not in a hurry to do last-minute shopping or wrap presents.

As the only child of an only child, she didn't exactly have a lot of family to buy gifts for—just her mother and her grandparents, Baba and Dida. She'd been organised enough to buy their presents weeks ago, although she would need to wrap them at some point before Midnight Mass later this evening. But still—she had plenty of time.

It was lucky, she supposed, that she'd had time

to stay back. If she'd left earlier, she would've missed the courier who'd knocked so frantically on the door. Not a normal courier, with a van and a uniform, but a courier in a suit, travelling in a jet-black sedan with darkly tinted windows. 'Courier' probably wasn't even the correct word—she suspected he actually had a far more important title, given his employers—but, regardless, he'd been desperate to deliver the letter that now lay before her on the information desk.

He'd also been very apologetic. He'd suggested he drive her somewhere quiet so they could talk, so she could read and digest what the letter contained. But, honestly, where was more quiet than a library?

And besides—she'd known. She'd known straight away what the letter meant.

She just hadn't expected what was inside it.

The courier—or maybe he'd said he was a valet?—had offered to stay while she read it, to answer her questions, but she'd shooed him away.

Now she almost regretted that. She had so many questions.

But they could wait.

Right now she just needed to be in the quiet of

this library. She needed to get her head around this news. She needed to begin to comprehend what this meant. Would she even be able to work here any more? Still live in her little apartment two blocks away? Did she even get the choice?

And what was that prickly heaviness in her chest? The moisture in her eyes?

How could she possibly grieve for a man she'd never met?

A frantic banging at the library door made Ana jump.

Her mother stood on the other side of the glass, wrapped in her favourite green winter coat, her gloved hands rattling the door. One hand held an envelope that matched Ana's.

'Ana!'

She rushed to let her mother in—it was cold, almost freezing outside.

The moment the door swung open the shorter woman threw herself into Ana's arms.

'Finally!' she said, as the door slammed shut behind her. 'Finally, my *bebo*, finally!'

They both held each other tightly, and when her mother finally stepped away tears had dampened Ana's white blouse.

But her mother's grief made sense. She'd lost the man she'd once loved. Once adored.

And now…now her mother was getting what she'd always wanted. Acknowledgement from the man Ana knew her mother had never stopped loving. Even as she'd hated him.

But for Ana? Ana had never really allowed herself to think too much about any of this. She'd just shoved it aside: her father wasn't part of her life, but her mother was, and she loved her enough for two parents. She hadn't let her thoughts wander to how he'd never wanted to meet her. Or, worse, how he'd never even acknowledged she existed. How he'd lied and denied that Ana was his daughter.

Well, she hadn't let her thoughts wander in that direction *often*, anyway. It was pointless and uncomfortable.

Her mother took a few steps away, snatching out a few tissues from the box on the corner of the information desk. She turned and handed them to Ana, and only then did Ana realise she was crying too.

She swiped at her tears, annoyed with herself for reasons she couldn't define.

'Prince Goran is dead,' Ana said in a low voice.

'Your *father* is dead,' her mother corrected. She still gripped the crumpled letter in her fist. Ana was sure it was also a letter from the Prince, just as she'd received. From her father.

'And you,' her mother continued, 'are now a princess. Princess Ana of Vela Ada.'

Princess Ana of Vela Ada.

Ana turned away from her mother, away from the library, and stared out into the darkness. She was at just the right angle to see the Christmas tree at the end of the street.

And as her tears fell, all the coloured lights and the perfect white star at the top blurred together.

Castelrotto, Italy

Rhys North's phone vibrated loudly, stirring him from his sleep.

He blinked at the time glowing green on the small digital clock on his bedside table: two a.m.

Adrenalin flooded his body. You didn't receive good news in the middle of the night. Rhys knew this incontrovertibly. You don't forget being shaken awake, or being told terrible news that made no sense, that didn't seem possible.

He hadn't forgotten the words that had changed his life, delivered just before three a.m. in a desert army camp: *'I'm so sorry, mate. There was nothing anyone could do.'*

But, he realised, his phone wasn't ringing any more. The vibration had stopped almost as soon as it started.

He reached out, flipping his phone over to look at its glowing face.

The tension in his shoulders eased.

His mum had sent him a message.

Merry Christmas, darling!! Hope you have a wonderful day. We all wish you were here! xx

She had, once again, forgotten the significant time difference between his home in Northern Italy and hers in Australia.

The phone vibrated again. Another message.

Oh, crap, I forgot the time again, darling! So sorry to wake you! Love you to the moon! xx

His mum wouldn't even have considered he'd slept through the first message, given she knew he'd become the lightest of sleepers in the four years since…

Rhys swung his legs over the edge of his bed and ran his hands through thick dark blond hair that was no longer buzz-cut-short. He was awake now, and he knew he wouldn't fall asleep again easily without doing something physical to take the edge off. He kept both his treadmill and the wind trainer for his bike set up in the living room of his villa. During the day, the floor-to-ceiling windows that covered two entire walls of the large room offered him views of the surrounding mountains, the Dolomites, but now all he could see was darkness.

Rhys never bothered closing his curtains—he wouldn't be much of a CEO of a security surveillance company if he allowed anyone close enough to look in without his permission.

On his treadmill, he barely warmed up before hitting the steepest incline setting and running as hard as he could, his bare feet slapping loudly in the silence. He ran until it hurt, and then ran some more, until finally he staggered off the machine, bare chest heaving, sweat drenching his skin.

Then he got into a cold shower and into bed, his skin still hot from such exertion.

He looked at his mum's message again:

Merry Christmas, darling!! Hope you have a wonderful day.

He didn't respond. He knew his mother wouldn't expect him to.

Because he never did. Yet still, like clockwork, his mother called, sent messages, even sometimes posted letters.

As if one day he'd turn back into the son he once was. The man he once was…

Before.

Before the night he'd been shaken awake.

Before the panic attacks.

Before he became practically a recluse here amongst the mountains.

Merry Christmas, darling!! Hope you have a wonderful day.

Well, he *wouldn't* have a wonderful day. He'd just have another day.

As it had been in the four years since he'd been shaken awake by his commanding officer, to be told of his young, healthy wife's sudden death, Christmas was just another day.

CHAPTER ONE

Present day...

ANA TOMASICH, PRINCESS OF VELA ADA, was gripping her wedding bouquet so tightly that her freshly manicured fingernails bit painfully into the skin of her palm.

But that was a good thing. That small sting of pain gave her focus. It silenced everything in her surroundings—her bridesmaids, who giggled at the foot of the stone steps that led into the church, the yells of the paparazzi, who stood behind specially erected barriers, and the constant click of their cameras. The hollow, tinny sounds from a row of flagpoles with flapping ropes and Vela Ada flags, and somewhere in the distance seagulls calling as they circled above the nearby beach.

In fact, the only thing that pain *didn't* silence was that soft, terribly polite voice she'd been ignoring for so long. The little voice inside her, standing square in front of her subconscious—the one she'd so determinedly pretended didn't exist.

Until now.

Now, in this new, perfect silence, that voice was loud.

Loud, and calm and absolutely, irrefutably, certain:

This is a mistake.

The sting in her palm eased. Her fingers, so tight and firm, loosened.

And in the silence—in the only moment Ana could remember feeling in control since she'd discovered she was a princess—she let her bouquet fall to the ground.

She imagined she heard it hit the footpath, but that was impossible.

Because, of course, it wasn't really silent.

Now she heard the noise. All the noise, and then even more noise, when, rather than retrieving her bouquet—as if dropping it had been an accident—she gave it a gentle kick to dislodge it from her satin-clad toes.

Her bridesmaids—colleagues from her old life at the library—hurried towards her, their faces matching studies of concern.

But she just shook her head, held up her

hand—she wanted them to stay put—and turned and got back into the vintage Daimler she'd only just exited, slamming the door behind her.

Her driver—one of the palace drivers—caught her gaze in the rear-vision mirror.

His gaze ever professional, he simply asked a question: 'Where to?'

'I don't care,' she said. 'Not here. Anywhere but here.'

She swallowed as the gravity of what she'd just done began to descend upon her shoulders.

Yet she had no doubts.

This was the right decision.

'Fast,' she added.

And with a satisfying screech of tyres her driver complied.

Hours later, the Vela Ada royal family's private jet landed at a small airport somewhere in Northern Italy. Ana didn't know exactly where, and she really didn't care. It was an irrelevant detail: being somewhere far from home was her number one priority.

Far from home, *very* far from the media and far from Petar.

Petar.

She could just imagine his fury once he'd realised he'd been left at the altar...

Actually, come to think of it, she couldn't.

As she was hastily rushed through passport checks and customs, far from where all the non-dignitaries had to queue, she digested the realisation that she actually couldn't say if Petar was the type of guy to shout and yell, or to be totally stoic, to try to cover for her, or blame her. She had no idea at all.

He certainly wouldn't have expected Ana to be a runaway bride. To be fair, Ana hadn't expected it either.

But she would have expected the man she was going to marry to notice she'd not been quite herself as the wedding had approached. She hadn't said anything, but surely Petar should have *known*. Surely he should have noticed she was saying the right things but deep down inside didn't really believe any of it. Shouldn't the person who loved you notice when things weren't right, even if you hadn't entirely realised it yourself?

Well, Ana had no *actual* personal experience to base that on, but she had a pretty good idea that was what love was about. She'd seen proper love before: in her grandparents, her friends.

In the movies, even. And she and Petar did *not* have it. She'd been an idiot to tell herself otherwise.

So here she was.

She hadn't really travelled much since Prince Goran had died. She'd initially felt rather fraudulent travelling as an international dignitary. She had, after all, spent twenty-nine years as a commoner, and certainly not a wealthy one. She was *normal*, and more used to budget airlines and cheap rentals than private jets, a security detail and VIP treatment.

But she was grateful for it now. Thanks to hastily managed diplomatic discussions, no one knew she was even in Italy, beyond trusted palace staff and select members of the Italian government. No one would be able to find her here. Not Petar. Not the media.

She was in a car now, white and nondescript. A member of her palace security detail was driving; another sat in the passenger seat. That was it—just the two.

She'd never had a full entourage of security personnel, unlike King Lukas and Queen Petra, or Lukas's brother, Prince Marko, and Marko's new wife, Jasmine. Not that Ana minded. She was absolutely comfortable with her status as a second-tier royal—the status she would've held even if Prince Goran *had* acknowledged her at birth. Partly because she was only the child of the late King Josip's brother, but also because Prince Goran had never really had a high profile in Vela Ada.

Was it because after his brother, King Josip, had his two children—Lukas and Marko—he'd felt the sting of being devalued to a very unlikely heir to the throne, after being the 'spare' for much of his life? Or maybe he'd been grateful not to be in the public eye? Ana had no idea. Her mother had never spoken about the type of man Goran had been—Ana suspected because her mother believed if you had nothing nice to say, you said nothing at all.

'You feeling okay, Your Highness?'

Ana met her driver's gaze in the rear-vision mirror and nodded. When his gaze swung back to the road, Ana's lingered on the mirror, and she realised the wedding make-up she still wore was smudged. She rubbed under her eyes in a half-hearted attempt to fix her appearance. But really it was a wasted effort. She was out of her wedding dress, at least, but she still wore her fancy bridal underwear beneath her jumper, coat and jeans. Her hair was still in an elaborate low bun too, although she'd tugged out the diamond-encrusted combs, causing loose strands of hair to hang haphazardly.

Anyway, did it really matter if she looked terrible? She'd just jilted her fiancé—she probably deserved to.

For the first time since she'd dropped her bouquet, she felt tears prickle. Annoyed, Ana moved her attention to the view outside the car.

All she could see was darkness. It was late November, and the sun had long set. Wherever they were, there were minimal street lights, and the sliver of a moon gave little away.

'Your Highness?'

This time it was the guard in the passenger seat. He was looking at her left hand, which she realised she was tapping loudly against the door handle. Did he think she was going to throw herself out of the moving car or something?

The idea made her grin, but her guard's hand moved to his seat belt, as if he was planning to throw himself across the luxury sedan to save her. She stilled her hand.

'*Oprosti.* I'm fine—really. Just a bit restless.'

He nodded but looked unconvinced.

Ana closed her eyes, resting her head against

the window. She still felt the guard's eyes on her. He was worrying about her.

As if *she* deserved someone whose entire job was to *worry* about her. *Her.* Ana Tomasich. Absolutely normal, no more interesting than anyone else, Ana Tomasich. She was a *librarian*, for crying out loud.

A librarian and a princess.

Princess Ana of Vela Ada.

Would the title ever sit comfortably on her shoulders? She couldn't imagine it. It just didn't seem to fit.

In fact, she'd been so certain it didn't fit when she'd first opened that letter from her father and seen what he'd done—how he'd finally acknowledged her birth and asked King Lukas to give her her 'rightful' title after his death—that she'd seriously considered declining.

She'd liked her life. She'd loved her career, her friends, her apartment. Why would she give all that up? And why would she put herself forward to be scrutinised and criticised? She knew there was a part of the Vela Ada population who'd be unwilling to embrace an illegitimate princess. She knew that her life would be different. And while she'd have money, and opportunities she could never have dreamed of, she would lose her privacy, and be giving up the life she'd lived for twenty-nine years.

In many ways her decision should've been easy—an easy *No, thanks!*—because it had been more than the practicalities of her decision that had loomed large for Ana. It had been the context of this 'gift' she'd been presented with.

Because when it came down to it, her father had waited until his death to acknowledge her.

And that made her feel incredibly small.

Her father had felt so strongly that he didn't want to deal with her—that he couldn't be *bothered* dealing with her—that he'd left her all alone to deal with this decision herself. He hadn't even bothered to ask her on his death-bed. He'd waited until he was gone. He'd kept all the answers to the questions Ana hadn't even known she wanted to ask from her. For ever.

So, yes. Part of her had wanted to tell the ghost of her father to shove his decision to make her a princess up his—

Anyway.

She hadn't.

She hadn't because this wasn't just about her. Her mother had fought for years for the palace to acknowledge Ana's existence, and she hadn't done it quietly. She'd paused in her crusade only when Ana had started kindergarten, when she'd been concerned about how Ana might be treated with such a scandal surrounding her. Her mother had always assumed Ana would pursue her father herself when she was older, but to her mother's surprise—and disappointment—that had never been a consideration for Ana. For Ana it was clear-cut—her father didn't want her. What was the point?

So when the decision to become a princess had so unexpectedly arisen, Ana's answer really hadn't been about what *she* wanted. It had been about her mother—it had been a public redemption twenty-nine years in the making.

And despite all that had happened since—the way her life had been turned upside down, leading to that moment outside that church—she couldn't say she regretted her decision.

But it still felt super-strange to be addressed as *Your Highness.*

The car slowed and turned off the smooth bitumen they'd been travelling on for well over an hour. Its wheels now crunched over gravel, its headlights the only illumination, as there hadn't been street lights for many kilometres. Tall trees flanked the narrow road—a driveway, maybe?—but as the car took twists and turns and climbed gradually higher Ana saw no clues to her destination.

Which was a *good* thing, Ana thought. The more secluded, the more private, the more remote the location the palace could find, the better.

Ever since she'd left that church all she'd wanted was to be away. Far away from her terrible decision to accept Petar's proposal instead of coming to her senses months ago. Or, better yet, coming to her senses when they'd first met, and she'd said yes to a date purely because he'd been gorgeous and charming and it had seemed crazy not to, rather than because she'd felt a spark of attraction.

But now that she *was* away—whisked off to a mountain in Northern Italy, no less—what did she *do*?

The car rolled to a stop.

A modern single-story house constructed mostly of windows sat just above the car, on the slope of a hill. It looked expensive and architecturally designed—the type of house you'd see on one of those fancy home-building TV shows that always go over budget. It was lit by a row of subtle lights that edged the eaves, and a brighter light flooded the entrance and the wooden steps cut into the hill that led to the front door.

There, at the top of the steps, stood a man.

Well, 'stood' was being generous. Really, he lounged, with one shoulder propped against the door frame and his long jean-clad legs crossed at the ankle.

He didn't move as her guards exited the car and opened Ana's door.

He didn't even move as Ana herself approached the bottom of the steps. He just stood there—*lounged* there—and studied her.

It said something about how much her life had changed that Ana noticed he didn't immediately jump to attention in her presence.

Oddly, it was kind of nice to have someone not clambering to impress her. Not treating her, baselessly, as more special than everybody else.

He *did* move, though, just before Ana climbed the first step.

He moved effortlessly, fluidly, like an athlete or a—what was it? A panther?

At that ridiculous idea Ana smiled for the first time that day. For the first time in days.

And by the time the man had swiftly descended the steps to greet her she was still smiling.

He met her gaze, taking in her smile. Then, for a moment, he smiled back.

He had a fantastic smile—a smile that made a face that seconds ago she'd subconsciously classified as just nice-looking to become handsome. With his slightly floppy hair, several days' stubble and rough-hewn cheekbones, he became *really* handsome, actually.

From nowhere, a blush flooded Ana's cheeks and an unmistakeable stomach-flipping jolt of attraction took over her body.

Then the man's smile fell away. In fact, it totally disappeared, as if it had never been there in the first place.

Shame warred with those still un-ignorable tingles that hadn't gone anywhere. *What sort of woman jilts her fiancé at the altar, then has the hots for a total stranger five minutes later?*

She straightened her shoulders, suddenly feeling totally aware of the elaborate lacy underwear she'd put on just hours ago for another man. It itched and chafed against her perfidiously heated skin.

Ana's smile had fallen away now too. The man looked at her with a gaze that was slightly bored, or inconvenienced. It was too dark out here for Ana to make out the colour of his eyes, but they were light. His hair was too. Even in the darkness it contrasted with the black of his coat. He must be blond, or his hair must be the lightest shade of brown.

He was tall too, Ana realised. She was wearing flat-heeled boots, but she was still slightly above average height for a woman, and yet she only came up to his shoulder. He was easily an inch or two over six foot. And broad. His winter clothing added breadth, but those shoulders weren't just the result of good tailoring.

She sensed him taking in her appearance: her camel-coloured coat, her chequered scarf, her jeans, her boots. And her dishevelled dark brown hair. Her messed-up make-up.

Maybe it was her embarrassment at the state she was in that made her snap a question at him:

'Who are you?'

He blinked. *'Žao mi je, ne govorim hrvatski,'* he said carefully, and in a foreign accent.

I'm sorry, I don't speak Croatian.

Vela Ada's native language was actually a unique Slavic dialect, but it borrowed heavily from neighbouring Croatia.

Usually she would've appreciated the effort to speak her language, but tonight she was just too tired—emotionally and physically exhausted—

and too sensitive to the bored judgment she could still see in the man's gaze.

'Who…' she said in English, in the most regal tone she could muster, 'are…' a long, pointed pause '…*you*?'

CHAPTER TWO

PRINCESS ANA WAS glaring at him. Her hands were on her hips, her eyes were narrowed and her full lips were in a perfectly straight impatient line.

It was quite late, but Rhys could see well enough in the muted light to acknowledge that Princess Ana was rather more attractive than he'd expected. Oh, he'd known she was pretty—but in person she was just...*more*. More *vivid*, somehow. More striking. Striking enough that he'd grinned at her like a moron for who knew how long—until he'd remembered he wasn't exactly thrilled to have a princess about to move in with him.

If anyone but Prince Marko had asked, he would never have agreed to it. He liked his privacy—he *needed* it, in fact. And he quite literally *guaranteed* it, with the most cutting-edge security system he'd designed protecting the perimeter of his property.

He *never* had guests.

He also didn't need the money the palace had offered. North Security was doing well. Extremely well, actually. This wasn't a financial decision.

But he had agreed. Because Marko wasn't one for asking favours. For Marko to call him so unexpectedly, Rhys knew this must be important to his friend. And when Marko had said it was Ana he was trying to help, Rhys hadn't been surprised.

Rhys remembered the scandal when Prince Goran had died last year, and Marko's subsequent guilt. His friend had been convinced he should have *known* he had a long-lost cousin, despite Rhys pointing out that the original saga— and Goran's denial of paternity—had all taken place well before Marko had turned ten.

But, regardless, Marko had a soft spot for Ana, and so when his new cousin had needed a place to escape to he had called the person best equipped to provide an absolutely secure, absolutely private location far from Vela Ada.

And because it was Marko who'd asked him—and because of that terrible night in the middle of the desert five years earlier—Rhys figured that a favour was the least he could do for the man who'd been there for him at his absolute worst.

Princess Ana gave a little huff of frustration. It was cold enough that it was accompanied by a tiny cloud of condensation.

'We should go inside,' he said, suddenly realising how cold he was. How cold they all must be.

The Princess's two guards were rugged up in black coats and beanies, but rather than encouraging their charge into the warm home they were clearly waiting for direction from Rhys. He had specified to Marko that he *must* be in charge of all security on the property should Ana come and stay with him, but this was ridiculous. No level of security was much use should they all freeze to death.

He turned on his heel and headed up the stairs. 'Follow me,' he said.

He heard the Princess grumbling behind him, but she could clearly see the wisdom in continuing their conversation indoors. She didn't meet his gaze again until they were inside. One of her guards had helped her shrug off her coat and scarf, and she was now sitting on the low, L-shaped fabric sofa in his living room.

She sat with excellent posture primly on the

edge of the seat. She wasn't meeting his gaze any more. Instead her attention flitted about the small space, not that there was a lot to see. He kept things pretty minimal, and the place was as tidy and streamlined as his interior designer had left it when he'd moved in almost five years ago.

Except for the treadmill and bike parked near the dining table, of course.

Rhys stood in front of her, now in T-shirt and jeans, after discarding his coat on the stand near the front door. 'My name's Rhys,' he said. 'Rhys North. I'm mates with Marko. We met when he took part in a training exercise with the Australian Special Forces about eight years ago. I've now left the regiment and I own a security company. Marko thinks you'll be safe here, and you will be. Does that answer your question?'

Ana's gaze met his again and she nodded.

'I assumed you'd been briefed, Your Highness,' Rhys said, belatedly remembering to address her correctly.

Ana looked at her guards, who stood there, ultra-professional, in standard bodyguard pose, their hands clasped in front of them. The two guards shared a quick glance.

'We did provide a briefing, Mr North… Your Highness,' one of them said, a moment later.

'However, it has been a very long and trying day—'

'Oh, *God*!' Ana exclaimed suddenly, cutting him off. 'Really? I'm *so* sorry.'

She sighed and twisted her fingers in a thick strand of dark brown hair that had fallen loose from what even Rhys could recognise as a wedding hairstyle.

'I honestly don't remember much since I left the church. Thank you for so politely excusing the fact that I've obviously totally ignored everything you've said to me. I've just been a *joy* today, haven't I? Jilting one man, ignoring others...' She buried her head in her hands.

Rhys interrupted her self-flagellation. 'Drink?' he asked.

Her dark head popped up instantly. 'Yes, please,' she said.

Then she flopped back onto his couch, resting her head on the back, her gaze trained on the ceiling.

A few minutes later—after directing the guards to the kitchen to help themselves to a drink and his limited selection of food—Rhys stood before her, drink in hand.

'Your Highness...?' he prompted.

Slowly she pushed herself forward until she

sat neatly at the edge of the couch again. She briefly met his gaze, and he couldn't miss the exhaustion and emotion in her eyes. She wasn't crying, though—didn't even look close to it.

'Ana,' she said. 'Please call me Ana.'

He nodded. 'You can address me as Mr North,' he said, very seriously.

Her eyes widened, and he watched her try to determine if he was joking.

A smile tugged at the corner of her lips. 'Okay,' she said, with the same mock-seriousness he'd employed. 'I will—Mr North.'

He smiled at her, meeting the sparkle in her gaze. He *liked* that sparkle, was *glad* he'd managed to elicit it from her.

'Rhys,' he clarified, 'is fine.'

She grinned. 'Oh, *no*, Mr North. I insist. About time someone else had an unnecessary title. *Vrag* knows, I'm sick of mine.'

'*Vrag?*' Rhys asked, as Ana took the squat ice-filled glass tumbler he handed her.

'The Devil,' she explained. Then took a long swallow of her drink. Instantly she coughed, slapping a manicured hand to her throat. 'What *is* this?' she asked.

'Gin,' he said.

'*Just* gin?'

He nodded. 'You look like you need a stiff drink.'

She smiled again and then took another, more measured sip. 'You, Mr North,' Ana said, 'are absolutely right.'

Ana watched Rhys as he walked over to the kitchen to talk to her guards. She wasn't at all surprised he was ex-military. In fact, he still looked absolutely fit enough to be serving. In his charcoal-coloured T-shirt the muscles of his biceps and arms were clear to see—so different from Petar's lean frame. Petar was very good-looking, but in a more sophisticated way than Rhys. He was all elegant lines and tailored suits, while Rhys looked rough and strong and practical—the kind of guy who'd carry you out of a burning office building rather than work inside it.

No.

She took another unwise gulp of her drink, wanting another punishing burn of alcohol to travel down her throat. Honestly, mere hours after running away from her fiancé was she really comparing him to another man? And finding her fiancé lacking.

She finished the drink. Even as the liquid

warmed her belly she felt like the worst person in the world.

Although she knew now—incontrovertibly—that she did not love Petar, and had never loved Petar, he didn't deserve having to wait at that church's altar for her never to arrive. To have the whole church witness that humiliation.

And it wasn't even just the church. With the wedding being televised, all of Vela Ada would know. He'd been dumped in the most public, most humiliating way possible.

And it was all her fault.

Yet she sat here, in a luxury home on a mountain, having an absolutely gorgeous man serve her drinks and make her laugh. She was being protected from the aftermath of her decision, and she knew it didn't reflect well on her that she was in no way regretting her decision to run as far away as possible.

She could not be in Vela Ada right now. She could not see Petar right now.

She needed some space to get her thoughts in order, to work out how she'd got to this point, how her *life* had got to this point.

But Petar did deserve an apology. And more than the swiftly written, utterly insufficient

I'm sorry she'd texted to him as the car had whisked her down that cobblestone street.

She stood and walked the short distance to the kitchen. The living space wasn't very large, and it was all open-plan—with the kitchen to one side, a long dining table in front of it and couches to its left.

All three men in the kitchen immediately turned to assist her. It was one of the nicer perks of being royalty—having people immediately pay attention to her. Quite different from her previous life, where she remembered being talked over in meetings or ignored by sales assistants. Although it did seem unfair that such courtesy wasn't offered to everyone...

'Excuse me,' she said in Slavic to her guards. 'I was just wondering where my phone and bags are.'

'We've put them in your room, Your Highness,' one of them replied.

She'd learnt long ago that palace staff would *not* just call her Ana.

Rhys seemed to have got the gist of the conversation. 'I'll show you your room now,' he said. He gestured down the corridor and followed close behind her.

There were only a few doors off the hallway, and he directed her into the first one.

The room wasn't large, but it had plenty of room for a queen-sized bed and a narrow writing desk against one wall.

'There's a private en suite bathroom through there,' he said, nodding to the far corner of the room. 'I chucked a few towels in there, but let me know if you need anything else. I'm not used to having guests up here, so there isn't any fancy soap, candles or potpourri and whatnot in there. Sorry.'

He did not look at all apologetic.

'I'll manage,' Ana said, and realised she was smiling again. How did Rhys *do* that? When he talked to her, it was as if she forgot everything that had happened today. Or this *year*, really.

They both stood in the doorway, and Ana was suddenly aware of how very close they were to each other. She had to tilt her chin up to meet his gaze, and she could actually smell him—the scent of his cologne or his deodorant or something—something clean and fresh.

She also registered the colour of his eyes for the first time: a dark blue that was almost grey. Outside, she hadn't been able to determine the colour of his hair, but when they'd walked in she'd realised it was a very dark blond. This close to him she could see more variation in the thick, shaggy hair—blond and brown and even a few strands of grey.

How old was he?

Her gaze travelled over his face. He had thick eyebrows and strong, quite full lips for a guy, though without even a hint of femininity. There were a few fine lines around his mouth and eyes. Stubble covered his sharp jaw, slightly darker than the hair on his head, and he was definitely the type of guy who suited that look.

She'd already imagined him being the kind of guy who'd rescue you from a burning building—a real hero type, befitting an ex-soldier— but this close to him, seeing his stormy eyes and the shadow of a beard, he looked almost... *dangerous.* There was a tension to his jaw, a steeliness to his gaze...

She realised, too late, that she was staring at him. Staring into that steely gaze. And he was staring right back.

Obviously she should look away, but she didn't. She couldn't.

His gaze was taking her in too, and the way it traced her features so intently made her feel incapable of movement. He took in her hair, her eyes, her nose, her lips…

What was he thinking?

Their gazes clashed again, and what she saw in his made her belly heat. Her whole body heat, actually.

Had she ever felt like this before? Reacted like this to a man before? Ana couldn't remember. She couldn't really think, to be honest. It was just so shocking to be drawn to this man she'd barely said anything to, whom she didn't know at all.

Her whole body itched to touch him. They hadn't touched since they'd met, she realised. They hadn't shaken hands… Nothing.

What would his skin feel like? Would it be hot, like hers felt right now? And how would it feel to have that big, strong body pressed against her…?

His gaze changed. It became empty, losing all that heat, all that connection. Just like he had outside in the cold, he'd switched off. He'd disappeared, as if that connection had never existed.

It was so abrupt as to feel almost physical. As if someone had dumped a bucket of snow over her head to snap her back to reality.

Reality.

Petar.

'Thanks for showing me my room, Mr North,' Ana said, forcing herself to put some distance between them and step into the room.

She fully intended to use his formal name from now on, and it wasn't a joke any more. Formality was good. It was *required*. She had no place flirting with this man. Apart from the fact she'd meant to share her wedding night with another man tonight, Rhys was also working for Marko, for the palace. This was all kinds of inappropriate.

'I need to phone my fiancé,' she said.

As she said *fiancé*, Rhys blinked. Or maybe she imagined he'd reacted.

In fact, his expression was so stony, so unreadable, it seemed plausible she'd imagined the entire past few minutes.

It would seem Rhys was keen to forget it had happened.

Good. She'd forget it too. No problem. This was an infinitesimal blip amongst the catastrophic screw-ups of the past twenty-four hours.

But as Rhys left her in her room, Ana had to work hard to ignore the little voice in her head—the little voice that had caused her *so* many problems today—that told her a man like Rhys North was not at all easy to forget.

CHAPTER THREE

ANA HAD BEEN in her room for over an hour—
easily enough time for Rhys to brief the palace guards on his property's security system,
including the mechanics of the fibre-optic perimeter sensors and state-of-the-art surveillance
cameras.

He'd had to tweak a few things—mainly because he generally reviewed the footage from
his many cameras only if he had a reason to,
but while Princess Ana was here one of the
guards would be monitoring the cameras 24/7.
Although in his five years here Rhys hadn't
seen anything more interesting on film than the
goatlike chamois and several curious birds—
the golden eagle his favourite—Marko wasn't
taking any risks, and therefore nor was Rhys.

When Ana finally emerged, Rhys had his
head in his fridge, trying to work out what on
earth he was going to feed a princess for dinner.

'Excuse me, Mr North?' she said, very politely.

Rhys took a step back so he could see her past the open fridge door. She looked different: she'd tidied her hair into a long ponytail that fell over one shoulder and she'd washed off the rest of her wedding make-up. It didn't look as if she'd put any more make-up on, and she'd lost her dramatic eyelashes and the perfect shape of her brows and lips, but she was still—and this was frustrating to Rhys—just as pretty.

The fridge started beeping at him for keeping the door open too long, and he slammed it closed with far more force than necessary, making Ana jump.

He didn't feel at all comfortable with what had happened in the doorway of her room. Or even earlier, when he'd first seen her. That had been easily dismissed—she was an attractive woman, who *wouldn't* gawk at her just a little? But in her room…it had felt pretty intense. Impossible to ignore.

He had *wanted* Ana. It had been a primal thing, a primal need—something he hadn't experienced in so very long he hadn't thought it was possible any more.

Sure, he'd *looked* at women since Jessica died, but he hadn't *needed* a woman. He certainly hadn't planned to be celibate for so long, but casual sex just didn't appeal—in fact, it felt somewhat disloyal to Jess just to sleep with some random woman.

Although he could just imagine Jess telling him he was an idiot, and could practically hear her voice telling him it was impossible to cheat on a dead person.

Jess had always been pragmatic. She never would have expected or wanted him to be single for the rest of his life.

But sex with Jess had been special. He'd slept with a few women before Jess, but it had never been with them as it had been with Jess. With other women it had been fun, but it hadn't been all-consuming. And now he'd experienced *more*, he didn't want to return to *less*.

And tonight… Tonight those moments with Ana had felt like *more*. Different from Jess, but equally intense. And that intensity had shocked him.

He hadn't been looking for it, and certainly hadn't expected to discover it with a woman he was being paid to protect.

And, more important, he wasn't sure if he *wanted* to want someone other than Jess. If, even after all these years, he was ready.

'Mr North?' Ana prompted.

'At your service,' Rhys said, with a deliberate grin. 'How can I help?'

Her gaze travelled over his face, but it wasn't the sensual exploration of before—now it looked as if she was trying to work out what was going on. Clearly his smile was not entirely convincing.

'Where are Adrian and Dino?' she asked.

'In the guest house,' he said.

'The *guest house*?' Ana squeaked, her eyes wide. 'Why would you have a guest house? You said you don't have many guests.'

He shrugged. 'I don't have any guests. It was here when I bought the place. The house only has two bedrooms—I guess the previous owner liked his own space as much as I do.'

'So we're *alone*?' Ana said, her voice still just a little higher-pitched than usual.

Her obvious discomfort helped Rhys relax a little. For some reason knowing they were both less than thrilled to be alone together helped.

Ana had had a big day—and, given she still called the guy she'd jilted her fiancé, maybe she was still in a relationship. Either way, pursuing anything with Ana given her current circumstances—regardless of the fact he was working for the palace—would be extremely uncool.

So maybe right now wasn't the time to be concerned about his wants and needs or whatever. There was no *maybe*, actually—there was no need at all.

Because nothing was going to happen between him and Ana.

Rhys ate dinner with Ana—which she hadn't really expected. But they didn't speak much while they ate, which suited her. The reality of the day required silence for her brain to begin to process it.

Had she really begun today planning to marry one man in Vela Ada and ended her day in a different country with another man altogether? Had she really done that? How had that happened?

Rhys had apologised for the lack of 'fancy' food. He'd heated up some lasagne he'd said he bought from a lady down in Castelrotto—the nearest town to Rhys's property—and cooked some frozen potato wedges in the oven, but it had been fine. Ana hadn't been in the mood for 'fancy' anyway. She didn't really feel she deserved it, given she'd probably caused the waste of the hundreds of fancy meals planned for her wedding reception.

She'd forgotten to ask Petar about that. She hoped that at least some of the food had been somehow repurposed. Maybe for a homeless shelter? Or maybe gifted to the army of staff who had worked at the reception venue?

Anyway, Ana *did* know that the reception hadn't gone on without her. She had naively hoped that maybe everyone had headed to the palace anyway, after it had been announced that the wedding wasn't happening. She'd imagined a great big party, everyone having a fabulous time without her, dancing to the live band, drinking all the very expensive champagne.

That idea had made her feel a little better— at least if the party had gone ahead, then she hadn't ruined the day for *everyone*. There'd been something salvaged from it.

But, no. Petar had said everyone had just gone home after they'd worked out that there really wasn't going to be a wedding.

'What would they have been celebrating?' he'd asked, incredulous.

Which was a fair comment, Ana acknowledged.

What she hadn't said in reply was: *They could've celebrated me realising just in time that marrying you would be a terrible mistake.*

Ana imagined a ballroom full of people, all dancing in celebration of Ana the Runaway Princess, maybe with balloons and streamers...

'May I ask what you're smiling about?' Rhys asked.

He'd pushed his seat back a little and relaxed into it. His plate was empty, his cutlery neatly placed diagonally.

Ana covered her mouth with her hand. 'I shouldn't be smiling,' she said. 'I hurt a lot of people today.'

Not only Petar, but her mother too. Her grandparents. Her friends.

'But you were smiling,' Rhys prompted. 'You have been for several minutes.'

How hadn't she noticed him looking at her?

She didn't know how to answer his question. As she'd said, she shouldn't be smiling. She shouldn't be feeling *happy*. She should be feeling bad. *Guilty.*

'Why do *you* think I'm smiling?' she threw back at him.

He folded his arms in front of his broad chest. 'I have no idea,' he said calmly. 'That's why I asked. I was curious.'

'I'd rather not say,' she said quickly. Then added, keen to change the subject, 'Where in Australia are you from?'

'Melbourne,' he said.

That was it—no further elaboration. They fell into another silence.

Ana realised that Rhys was waiting for her to finish her meal before leaving the table, which was very polite of him. She knew she should tell him he didn't need to wait for her—given she had so unexpectedly turned up at his doorstep, she could hardly expect him to be an attentive host. But she didn't.

She *liked* having Rhys sitting at the table with her. She liked *him*, she realised. On a day that was definitely a low point in her life, he'd managed to make her smile—more than once.

Sure, she'd freaked out a bit when she'd realised they'd be alone in his house together, but it was clear now that nothing was going to happen between them. She hadn't been able to interpret his expression when she'd first walked into the kitchen, after her call with Petar, but it had certainly held none of the heat from before.

But it wasn't that stony emptiness he seemed to so easily switch to either—that expression that gave nothing away.

If anything, she would have said he looked sad.

But that didn't seem to fit with this strong, handsome, confident man—and she'd seen no evidence of sadness since.

She must have imagined it.

'My fiancé seems to think I just have cold feet,' she said suddenly.

Rhys's expression was instantly uncomfortable. 'You want to talk about your fiancé with *me*?'

Ana shrugged. She needed to talk to *someone*. 'You asked why I was smiling. I thought you might be interested.'

'That was because you have a nice smile—not because I want to know the details of your relationship.'

The casually spoken compliment did not go unnoticed, and Ana fought the blush that crept up her neck. She kept on talking in an effort to ignore it. 'I just thought it was weird,' she continued. 'I thought he should know I wouldn't do something so dramatic on a whim.'

Rhys didn't say anything, but equally he didn't

get up, even though she'd now also arranged her cutlery in the 'finished' position.

'He was incredibly calm on the phone before. If someone did that to me, I'd be *really* angry. Wouldn't you?'

Rhys shrugged, non-committal.

'He was all kind and patient and supportive. And you know what's also weird?' Ana didn't wait for an answer—not that she expected one. 'He didn't seem particularly hurt. He made the conversation all about *me*—about how I must have felt so stressed, and overwhelmed, and how so much has happened in my life in the past twelve months, blah-blah-blah...' She sighed. 'Not that I *want* him to be feeling terrible, but I expect *I* would. I mean, I *know* I would if the man I loved didn't turn up to our wedding.'

Ana looked down at her fingers as she absently traced the curved edge of her dinner plate. Her nails still looked immaculate, yesterday evening's French manicure remaining perfect and unchipped.

'It actually makes me a bit angry, really, that he was so calm,' Ana realised. 'If he cared about me, he'd...well, *care* more.'

'Maybe he prefers to keep his emotions close to his chest,' Rhys said.

Ana's gaze jerked up to meet his gaze. 'Or maybe he's just continuing to be the perfect fiancé he always has been.'

She knew she didn't make it sound as if that was a good thing.

'You don't *want* a perfect fiancé?' Rhys asked.

'No one's perfect,' Ana said. 'But Petar has done everything in his power to pretend to be. Today I finally stopped lying to myself. Petar is prepared to do anything to become a member of the Vela Ada royal family. He's never *loved* me.'

Despite acknowledging to herself that she didn't love her fiancé, and subsequently realising today that Petar didn't love her either, saying it out loud made it all real.

And that hurt.

Her gaze fell back to her plate as hot tears prickled.

'It was always too good to be true,' she said. 'A man like Petar would never have wanted someone like me if I wasn't a princess. Even today, after I've humiliated him, he's still doing everything he can to change my mind. The way he's reacted is supposed to be endlessly understanding and romantic, but really it's all a total farce.'

Rhys murmured something that sounded a bit rude under his breath, but Ana didn't quite catch it.

'Pardon me?' she asked.

He shook his head. 'Nothing,' he said.

Ana straightened her shoulders and then pushed back her chair, ready to stand.

'Wait,' he said. He met her gaze and held it. 'You made the right decision.'

'How do you know that?' Ana asked. 'Because I can tell *you* know you did—even if you haven't realised it yet,' he said. 'And also, a guy who is sitting back in Vela Ada, rather than doing everything in his power to find you, to try to change your mind? Well, he's not the right guy. He doesn't deserve you if he won't fight for you.'

After her day—and the confusing maelstrom of guilt and hurt and disappointment that continued to whirl within her—it was the perfect thing to hear.

And he was right. She could regret hurting people, but she couldn't regret finally coming to her senses.

'Thank you,' she said, and it would have been so easy to lose herself in the depths of his blue-grey gaze. In the gaze of a man she had no doubt *would* fight for the woman he loved. But instead she stood, and then added, '…Mr North.'

CHAPTER FOUR

IT TOOK HOURS for Ana to fall asleep.

Her thoughts weren't particularly coherent as exhaustion warred with her overthinking, but they centred mostly on her immediate family: her mother and grandparents. How must *they* be feeling?

Her mother had sent her several text messages, but she'd responded to only one, just to reassure her she was okay and would be home in a few days' time.

Her mother would be devastated. She'd fought for years for Ana to be acknowledged by the royal family, and now that she had been, her mother was convinced Ana's life was perfect. Petar had been a natural progression of that perfection—the living embodiment of all of her mother's dreams come true.

Ana could see now that she'd bought into it too—that she'd allowed herself to be swept up in Petar and the idea she was living a fairy-tale happy-ever-after.

Their engagement, and then agreeing to a televised wedding—it had all been part of Ana's fantasy life. The life that her mother had always dreamed of for her only daughter.

Maybe that was why she'd allowed it to go so ridiculously far, despite her reservations—which she *had* had, no matter how well she'd repressed them. Maybe she'd just wanted to make her mother happy.

But that felt like such a cop-out. Ana was her own woman. She alone was ultimately responsible for dating Petar, for accepting his proposal and for actively organising her own magazine-spread wedding.

She'd done all that, and now, as she tossed and turned in a strange bed in the mountains of Northern Italy, she was no closer to working out why...

Thanks to the heavy blackout curtains in her room, it was dark when Ana eventually woke from a dreamless sleep. She had a shower, got dressed in jeans and a T-shirt, and headed out into the kitchen.

It was mid-morning, and the curtains that had

covered the walls of windows last night had all been pulled aside, revealing the remarkable view the house offered of the surrounding Dolomites. And what a spectacular view it was—all snow-capped mountain ranges and emerald tree-filled vistas that rolled and dipped. Even though it was November, the sun was bright today, showcasing the stunning view in perfect, postcard-worthy light.

However, Ana didn't spend a particularly long amount of time admiring the view, as just at her left she had an alternative view on offer.

Rhys North, jogging on his treadmill.

His back was to her as he ran, his attention focused on the view in front of him.

He wore a loose sleeveless T-shirt that revealed arms and shoulders heavy with muscle, and knee-length jogging shorts. All his clothing was dark with sweat, which possibly should have been unattractive, but somehow Rhys managed to make sweat seem virile and strong.

He must have heard her, because he punched a button on the treadmill's console and slowed to a walk.

He turned to catch her gaze over one shoulder. 'Just need to cool down,' he said.

Ana walked up to him. 'Good morning,' she said.

He grinned a greeting. 'Good morning to you too.'

'Sorry about last night,' Ana blurted out suddenly. 'I shouldn't have rambled on about all that stuff. You're my bodyguard, or my hotelier or something—'

'Security consultant,' Rhys interjected helpfully, with another grin.

'Okay,' Ana said. '*Security consultant.* But that definitely doesn't require you to play psychologist or counsellor. I'm sure you didn't want to hear all the messy details of my relationship.'

He shrugged. 'I didn't mind.'

He pushed another button and the treadmill came to a stop. He then unselfconsciously used the bottom of his shirt to clear his brow of sweat, the action revealing what seemed like hectares of muscular abdominal ridges.

Oh, my.

Rhys honestly hadn't planned to do that. It had been an automatic action, but seeing Ana blush as she took in his chest and stomach made him glad he had. He was human, he had an ego and he worked damn hard to stay this fit… So, yes, it felt *good* to see that Ana liked what she saw. Really good.

He took longer than necessary to wipe his face—which probably made him a very bad person, given nothing had changed as far as the situation between him and Ana. She'd just ended a relationship. He was protecting her.

But he couldn't help himself.

It was just like those long minutes in her room…magnetic and addictive. And all the more so because he *knew* nothing would happen. He didn't have to worry about Jess, or about how he'd feel being with a woman other than his wife. He didn't need to deal with any of the complicated stuff—he needed only to experience this undeniable snap and tension between him and the Princess.

As he dragged his shirt back down, Ana jerked her gaze towards the window.

'Amazing,' she breathed.

Seriously?

He grinned. 'Well, I'll take that—'

She whirled to face him, muttering a string of Slavic curses to herself. 'I meant the *view*, Mr North,' she said firmly.

He was starting to really like her insistence on addressing him so formally. It felt like a shared joke, almost intimate—it certainly wasn't putting space between them, as he knew she intended it to.

She was staring with determination at his face, not allowing her gaze to drift.

'Christmas must be wonderful here, Mr North,' she said.

'Christmas?' he asked, thrown by the change of subject.

She clasped her hands primly in front of her. 'Yes,' she said. 'Christmas. I believe Castelrotto is famous for how beautiful it is at Christmas time. I couldn't sleep last night, so did a bit of research about where I'm staying, and Christmas is clearly a big thing here. There's a Christmas market that starts in a few weeks—during Advent. Is it as enchanting as all the tourist websites say?'

Rhys stepped off the treadmill and headed to the kitchen for a drink of water.

'I wouldn't know,' he said, quite stiffly.

She followed him. 'Really? I'd imagine you'd need to go to quite a bit of effort to avoid it, given how small the town is.'

He filled a tall glass with water. 'I don't avoid

the market,' Rhys said. 'I just don't pay much attention to anything to do with Christmas.'

She was looking at him, curiosity wrinkling her forehead. She'd kept her hair down today, and it hung in heavy waves over her shoulders. It would be much easier to answer with a white lie—Ana would have neither known nor cared if he'd just agreed that the market was, in fact, enchanting.

'I *adore* Christmas,' Ana said. 'I always have.' She paused, then said carefully, 'Do you not have a family to celebrate with?'

He downed the water in a series of long swallows, really hoping that Ana would walk away. But of course she didn't.

Here was another opportunity to lie—as Ana had pointed out, it wasn't his role to play counsellor or psychologist. Equally, it wasn't his role to spill his guts.

'I have a big family back in Australia,' he said. 'A sister, a brother, great parents and a wonderful extended family. Christmas was incredible when I was growing up—my parents have a huge pool in the backyard and we'd host a barbecue for the whole family and anyone who had no one else to celebrate with. It was great. I loved it.'

So he didn't lie.

What *was* it about this woman?

He knew the question she was going to ask next.

'What happened?' she said.

The sympathy in her eyes almost made him leave the room. He'd *never* wanted this—never wanted people to feel sorry for him. To pity him. Yet to this woman who'd exposed her own vulnerability to him last night he found he could be nothing but honest.

'My wife died,' he said simply. 'And everything changed.'

CHAPTER FIVE

'I'LL JUST GO take a shower,' Rhys said into the stunned silence, as Ana struggled to work out what to say. What *could* she say?

But she didn't need to work it out, because only moments later she was alone.

'My wife died.'

Ana had not expected Rhys to say that. Although, on reflection, it had been stupid to ask him what had changed: he'd clearly had an idyllic childhood, so something *had* to have gone catastrophically wrong for his view of Christmas to change so dramatically.

'My wife died.'

Ana walked into the kitchen and searched through the overhead cupboards for a mug and in the large walk-in pantry for some coffee. Then she stared out at the view as the kettle boiled.

'My wife died.'

She would never have guessed Rhys had ever

been married—he had the cocky confidence of a handsome perennial bachelor, in no hurry to settle down. And, besides, he lived alone in a two-bedroom home in the middle of nowhere—albeit a spectacularly picturesque middle of nowhere.

But not the type of place that screamed wife and family, or even kids.

The water had boiled, so Ana poured herself a strong coffee, with only a dash of milk from the fridge, and took a seat at the breakfast bar, angling her stool so she still faced the view.

Immediately outside the house the ground sloped away in a rolling curve of thick grass, liberally sprinkled with tiny yellow flowers. It undulated for a while, before merging with a dense forest, and then beyond the forest sat the angular, brutal shapes of the surrounding mountains—the tallest with a mantle of snow.

From here, Ana couldn't see another building—certainly not another person. It was the perfect place to hide for a runaway bride.

Or for a grieving husband.

Her throat was tight and prickly, her coffee forgotten in her hand, when Rhys strode back into the room.

She met his gaze, and Rhys's eyes immediately narrowed in response. 'Please don't,' he said.

'Don't what?' she asked.

'Feel sorry for me.'

'I can't even begin to imagine—' Ana said.

He shook his head, silencing her. 'Please,' he repeated. 'Don't.'

Ana nodded.

He caught her gaze again. 'Her name was Jessica. It was five years ago,' he said in clipped tones. 'Sudden. Brain aneurysm.' A pause, then a shrug of his broad shoulders. 'People tend to want to know the headlines.'

He was right, she had been curious. She started to open her mouth to say something—but he silenced her again with only a look.

He was right to do so. She had been about to say something empty—albeit heartfelt—and sympathetic.

But what to say instead?

Ana noticed for the first time that he had a small backpack slung over one shoulder, and as she watched he headed for his coat rack and retrieved a pair of boots from its base.

'I'm going for a walk,' he said.

'Can I come?' Ana asked.

* * *

Rhys hadn't expected Ana to want to join him and he very nearly said no.

But instead he shrugged. 'If you want.'

He'd spent a lot of time hiking through the mountains of Seiser Alm after he left the regiment. He'd hiked alone, and as he'd walked he'd spent time in his own thoughts, in his own grief.

But then one day, a few months after he'd moved to Castelrotto, he'd arrived home from his hike, his brain buzzing with an idea he'd had about starting his own security business—about transferring his military expertise to private security systems and consulting. And he'd realised he hadn't thought of Jess the entire time.

At the time, his guilt had made him cry. Cry with his head in his hands on the steps of this house he'd bought that was *nothing* like the home he'd had with Jess back in Melbourne. Cry as he hadn't since the day Jess had died.

But later he'd realised it had been a turning point. And now it was his new normal—he still loved Jess, he still grieved for Jess and sometimes all he could think of was her. But at other times he thought of other things.

That was his life now. Sometimes he thought

of Jess. Often he thought of all sorts of other things.

But never another woman.

Until now.

The woman in question, now dressed in coat, boots and a red knitted beanie, walked beside him as they crossed the meadow that stretched between his home and the mountain range.

'Predivan...' Ana said softly.

'Pardon me?' Rhys asked.

Ana stopped walking so she could slowly spin in a circle to take in the entire landscape. 'Wonderful,' she translated. 'This place is wonderful. I've never been anywhere like it before.'

'Really?' Rhys asked. 'You've never been skiing in the Dolomites?'

Rhys had discovered Castelrotto when Marko had taken him skiing at nearby Cortina d'Ampezzo, in a misguided attempt to cheer him up shortly after the abrupt end of his military career. Marko had grown up skiing at glamorous Cortina—surely Ana had too?

Ana's lips quirked upwards. 'Remember I'm only a very *recent* princess? I've never actually been skiing. The last time it snowed in Vela Ada was before I was born, so I haven't even *seen* snow.'

Rhys raised his gaze in the direction of the nearby snow-capped mountains.

'You know what I mean,' she said, grinning. 'Close enough to touch. To make a snowman or a snow angel.'

'Or have a snowball fight?' Rhys suggested.

Ana's eyes lit up at the idea. 'Oh, yes! *Exactly.* I want to try out all things snow-related.'

They started walking again.

'I had forgotten you weren't always a princess,' Rhys said.

Ana slanted a gaze at him. '*I* haven't,' she said. 'I keep expecting to wake up one day and feel like one, but it hasn't happened yet.'

The ground had started to slope upwards, and they headed along a path Rhys took often enough to have worn a dirt track amongst the lush grass.

'What *should* a princess feel like?' Rhys asked.

Ana shrugged. 'I wish I knew,' she said. 'Not like me.'

'Why not you?'

She stopped in her tracks, only a few steps before the forest began in earnest, listening to the needles of the tall Norwegian Spruce trees rustling in the breeze.

'Why *anyone*?' Ana said. 'Isn't it just crazy

that one random person gets all this prestige, and fancy houses and money, purely because of who their parents are, and another random person gets nothing?'

'You don't feel you deserve it,' Rhys said. It was a statement, not a question.

Ana just nodded and continued along the path. It got rockier in the forest, and they both needed to concentrate on where they placed their feet.

'How about all the good that the Vela Ada royal family do?' Rhys asked. 'With the island's political unrest over the past few years, its royal family has played an important role in unifying the country, don't you think?'

It had been government corruption that had finally dragged his friend Marko back to Vela Ada and an active role as Prince. Although there was no doubt that his wife, Princess Jasmine, had also played a part, the royal family was now more popular than ever—because they had been there at a time of turmoil. Stable and solid, as they had been for hundreds of years.

Ana looked as if she was going to argue, but he pressed on before she could.

'You know Marko feels very similarly to you, right? I've heard all this before—about how un-comfortably privilege sits on his shoulders, how stupid it is that he gets so much for the act of simply being born.'

The path had started to climb upwards, winding between larger rocks and boulders.

'But the fact is, he *is* a prince. You *are* a princess. Rather than whining about being so unbelievably fortunate, you should *do* something with all that privilege.'

He knew all too well that there were far worse burdens than a royal title.

Ana stopped walking abruptly and turned to face him. Too late, Rhys realised that this *wasn't* like arguing with Marko—his friend whom he had told to pull his head in more than once. He was supposed to be working for Princess Ana. *Serving* her, really. She wasn't an old friend. She was a woman he'd just met—who also happened to be a princess he'd been hired to protect.

'For your information, Mr North,' she said coldly, 'I have been doing quite a lot with my privilege. It's the reason I ultimately accepted my royal title—so I could draw attention to charities I feel passionate about—mostly related to literacy. I've also started my own project that aims to bring library services to older Vela Adians—initiatives like library services for nursing homes and funding for more talking books and…'

Her strident words petered out and she shoved her hands into the pockets of her coat.

She sighed. 'But you are right. I *should* just get on with being a princess rather than debating my worthiness for the role. Embrace my good fortune rather than question it. It's just that…'

She paused for long moments.

'Just that…?' Rhys prompted.

Her expression shifted from defiant to defeated. 'Well, it's kind of difficult *not* to question whether I deserve any of this—if I *deserve* to be whisked across Europe in order to escape my own wedding—when my own father determined that I *wasn't* worthy of being a princess for the first twenty-nine years of my life.'

Ana turned on her heel and continued up the path at a brisk pace.

Rhys followed equally briskly. 'Ana, wait.' He'd never intended to cause such pain in her eyes. 'I'm sorry. I shouldn't have—'

'No,' Ana said, interrupting, her gaze still on the path ahead of her. Her breathing was heavier now as she negotiated the slope. 'You're right. I *do* need to stop overthinking this. I'm a princess now. That's not changing. I need to deal with it and move on. Focus on all the good stuff—the charity work I can dedicate myself to, the fact that my mum will never need to worry about money for the rest of her life. The fact that there's a royal hairdresser and my hair has *literally* never looked so good.'

Her lips twitched in the briefest smile.

'I should ignore the rest. The scrutiny by the public and the media. The fact that I had to give up a career I loved and an apartment I scrimped and saved for that symbolised years of hard work and then suddenly became cheap and disposable. And the fact that I gave up the chance to live a normal, *private* life...'

Rhys was keeping up easily, used to these trails and fitter than her. But his concentration was focused on her, not on where he was going, so it was probably unsurprising that he stepped on a loose rock, turned his ankle and suddenly found himself crashing towards the ground.

He hit it hard, and with a loud grunt, landing only a few feet from Ana's boots.

'Rhys!' Ana exclaimed, retracing her steps to crouch beside him.

It was the first time she'd said his name. He

liked the way it sounded on her lips—her accent making the single syllable rich and husky.

She immediately realised her mistake. 'Mr North,' she corrected herself. 'Are you okay?'

He assessed the damage: none, apart from the bruise that would eventually develop on the hip that had taken the brunt of his fall. And, of course, the bruise to his pride.

He shifted his weight until he was sitting up. 'I'm fine,' he said. 'Totally fine.'

Ana rearranged her own legs until she sat beside him.

'I'm sorry,' Rhys said. 'I know the royalty are under a lot of pressure—I've been Marko's friend for almost a decade. I know it's real, and I know it's hard. Especially for you, given your unusual circumstances. I shouldn't have called you a whiner—that was unfair.'

Ana shook her head. 'You were speaking the truth. I *am* a princess now. So, however I feel, *that* is how a princess feels.' She grinned. 'If I keep reminding myself, eventually it will stick.'

Rhys smiled at Ana.

'If it helps, I've never doubted that you're a princess, Your Highness.'

Ana smiled back.

'Why, thank you, Mr North.'

CHAPTER SIX

THEY DIDN'T TALK much for the rest of their hike, which suited Ana fine.

It was a comfortable silence, and often a *necessary* silence—for Ana, at least, who was not particularly fit—as they traversed the more challenging inclines of their hike.

When they eventually arrived back at Rhys's house, and Ana had showered, she curled up on Rhys's couch to read one of the dozens of books she had on her e-reader. It was a Sunday, but Rhys spent the rest of the day working in his study, except for frequent trips to the kitchen to brew a never-ending succession of cups of coffee.

Halfway through a book she was barely paying attention to, Ana finally convinced herself that she could, in fact, manage a call to her mother. After all, what was the worst that could happen?

As it turned out, the worst was pretty bad.

'How could *you?'* was the dominant theme. How could she humiliate the man she loved like that?

Her mother didn't want to hear Ana challenge the whole 'love' situation.

How could she throw away the opportunity to marry Petar Kovacic?

As if Petar was the most perfect of men.

And—most tellingly—how could she do something like that in front of literally *everyone* in Vela Ada?

Her phone call with Petar had been uncomfortable and frustrating. But this call... This call exposed her mother's hurt and left Ana's shoulders heavy with guilt and regret. Not for running away from Petar, but for the pain she'd caused the woman she loved most in the world.

'Are you okay, Ana?'

Rhys's voice made Ana startle. She realised she'd been staring at the black screen of her phone ever since she'd ended the call to her mother. She hadn't noticed Rhys re-enter the room.

She was still sitting cross-legged on the plush couch, and she untangled her legs and stood. 'Of course,' she said brightly.

She walked over to the kitchen. Earlier Dino

had gone into Castelrotto for supplies, and Ana had made up a cheese platter that she and Rhys had been grazing on throughout the afternoon. She stood at the granite counter and calmly sliced off a chunk of taleggio cheese and placed it on a cracker.

Rhys walked over so he stood on the opposite side of the bench. 'Are you sure?'

Ana looked up to meet his gaze. She forced a grin. 'Yes,' she said firmly.

As Ana watched, Rhys sliced his own piece of cheese. He'd chosen one of the hard cheeses—pecorino, Ana thought—and he ate it just like that: no cracker, no crusty Italian bread.

Ana only realised she was watching him chew and swallow when her gaze met his eyes—and his raised eyebrows.

'Really, *really* sure?'

How did he do that? He was teasing her, making her lips curve in a genuine grin even as her brain was lecturing her on the million mistakes she'd made that had led to what had happened yesterday.

When he was like this—when he had that thoughtful sparkle in his gaze—he was impossible to ignore. And it was *so* tempting to talk to him, but—

'I thought we'd established that you don't need to be my counsellor,' Ana said. 'I don't expect you to listen to all my woes.'

He shrugged. 'Yeah, well, I didn't expect to have a princess living with me—and I'm sure *you* didn't expect to be living with a widower who doesn't like Christmas—so I think we can both agree this is an unusual situation.'

Ana was still unconvinced. 'You don't want to hear my problems.'

His eyes narrowed. 'How about *I* decide that?' he said.

He skirted around the bench and grabbed a bottle of wine from one of the overhead cupboards.

'Would you like a glass of Chianti to accompany that cheese you're not eating?'

Ana found herself nodding, but rather than eating her forgotten cheese she placed it on the edge of the wooden platter. She'd lost her appetite.

He poured her a glass and pushed it across the granite towards her. He propped his hip against the counter, his own glass held loosely in his fingers. In getting the wine he'd had to move closer to her, and now he wasn't much more than a metre away.

It was a reasonable distance—he certainly wasn't crowding her—but Ana felt his proximity with every bone in her body.

They still hadn't touched. Even when he'd fallen in the woods he'd ignored her proffered hand and stood unassisted.

Ana's attention dropped to Rhys's fingers, which absently twisted his wine glass to and fro.

How would it feel to have those fingers against her skin...?

As that was *not* where Ana wanted her thoughts to be heading, she grabbed hard onto a topic guaranteed to distract her from Rhys's size, and strength, and general gorgeousness.

Her mother.

'My mum went through a lot when I was born,' she blurted out.

Rhys nodded. 'I've heard part of the story from Marko.'

'I don't know much of the detail of her relationship with Prince Goran, but I know she loved him. He was older, he was married and she knew she shouldn't—but she loved him anyway. When he refused to acknowledge my paternity, it broke her.'

Ana took a sip of her wine, closing her eyes to gather her thoughts.

'He told her the baby couldn't possibly be his, but as there was no one else my mother always knew the truth. At first she kept things private, but when Prince Goran began to ignore her calls he made it impossible for her. So she went to the press.'

Ana took another long drink of wine. She hadn't even been born yet, but the injustice of what had happened to her mother still made fury and disappointment war inside her. How could her father have been so cold?

'It was a huge scandal at the time—splashed all over magazines and newspapers. My mother even did a few television interviews. All she wanted was a paternity test, but with no concrete proof of their relationship—no photos, nothing—the Prince got away with dismissing my mother as a liar. It must have been beyond awful for her.'

Ana looked down and realised she'd finished her wine. She placed her glass on the counter.

'A lot of people *did* believe my mother. It could have been resolved by a paternity test, and because the Prince refused it raised suspicion. But Goran's unblemished history—both before and after—made him seem a man unlikely to have an affair. In the end the palace's refusal to engage with someone they saw as a delusional woman was the narrative that won out. And eventually she gave up.'

She met Rhys's gaze. He'd barely drunk any of his wine. She was tempted to ask for some more. She wasn't usually a big drinker, but the wine was delicious—warm and comforting.

But she decided being in any way less inhibited around Rhys was probably a terrible idea. Despite talking exclusively about her mother, he had become no less deliciously handsome to her recalcitrant libido.

Instead she refocused on the cheese platter and sliced off another chunk of cheese she had no plans to actually consume.

'For Prince Goran to finally acknowledge me, for me to become a princess…that was *everything* to my mother. For her, it was redemption. People had never forgotten what she'd claimed all those years ago, and Prince Goran's denial followed her everywhere. For me to become Princess Ana—that was *her* victory.'

'That's why you accepted the title?' Rhys said.

'Yes,' Ana said simply.

'You didn't want it for yourself?'

'No,' she said, even more quietly. 'I didn't.'

She swallowed. She'd picked up a cracker at

some point and was turning it over and over in her fingers.

'I think that's what went wrong this past year. My decision to become Princess Ana wasn't my own, and it was as if all my subsequent decisions haven't been entirely mine either.'

Ana stilled her hands and straightened her shoulders.

'But I own that now. I was trying to be the perfect princess—for my mother, mostly, but also for my grandparents and for myself. I've not had a father all my life. I wanted to show Vela Ada what he missed out on. And to do that I had to be perfect. But perfect isn't me.'

The cracker snapped into two in her hand. Ana stared at the pile of crumbs in her palm.

'And now I've shamed my mother again by running away,' she said quietly. 'She had no idea how I really felt about Petar. No idea how I felt about being a princess. I've blindsided her and I've embarrassed her—in *public*, no less. She didn't deserve for this to happen. For something like this to happen to her *again*.'

'You couldn't marry a man you didn't love,' Rhys said, his voice low.

He'd moved closer, but Ana kept her attention trained on her hands.

'Why not?' she said. 'I dated a man I didn't love. I accepted his proposal. I had a million opportunities to walk away and I took none. What does that say about me?'

'It says you've had a very confusing year,' Rhys said.

Ana shook her head. 'That's just an excuse.'

'No, it's an explanation,' Rhys said. 'Your life has been turned upside down. You've been under a lot of pressure.'

Ana dumped the pile of crumbs on the bench, then brushed her hands against her jeans. 'I'm just so angry with myself for letting this happen. What was I even *thinking*? It's like I got so caught up in the idea of being the perfect Princess that when the perfect Prince turned up it was impossible to say no.'

She rubbed at the place where her engagement ring had sat for the four months leading up to her wedding day. Now it was in a safe somewhere in the palace.

'But that's not *me*,' Ana said firmly. 'It's not me to get swept up in something and ignore all my own internal warning systems. Usually I'm super-cynical in a new relationship. I used to think it was because of what happened to my mother, which would make sense, but then how do you explain me almost *marrying* a guy I didn't love and who clearly didn't love me?'

Ana looked up from her hands to discover Rhys had moved closer. After their hike he'd showered and changed into a deep green T-shirt that clung to his shoulders and biceps and made his eyes seem impossibly blue.

'I don't think everything needs an explanation, Ana,' he said. 'But, for what it's worth, it sounds like you were trying so hard to do the right thing by everyone—even yourself, in a misguided way—that you lost sight of what you actually wanted.'

Ana's laugh was dry. 'Today I think I want to go back to being a librarian. To living in my apartment. To knowing what I actually *want.*' She sighed. 'Because right now I have absolutely no idea what that is.'

Her gaze had been roaming aimlessly about his shoulders, mostly avoiding his gaze as she'd been talking. But now, as she contemplated what she *wanted*, it was impossible not to be drawn back to his eyes.

And then just to look at him. To look at the man who'd just so patiently listened to her share more than she'd ever told another soul.

Although, to be truthful, it wasn't his listening skills that she found herself admiring now. That she found herself *wanting* now.

They'd looked at each other like this before. When she'd arrived, on the steps to his house. And again in the doorway of her bedroom.

Both those times he'd eventually shut her out—shut down the connection and doused the heat in his gaze so effectively it was as if it had never existed.

But he hadn't shut down anything this time.

Something told her that he wouldn't.

Or he couldn't.

'Ana—' he started, then swallowed. 'I mean, Your Highness—'

'You got it right the first time… *Rhys*,' Ana said, emphasising his name. She liked the way it sounded on her tongue. Why on earth had she insisted on calling him Mr North?

Distance. That's right.

He shook his head. 'I don't think this is a good idea. You've had a rough few days. You've been drinking—'

'*One* drink, Rhys. I'm not even tipsy. And, yes, I *have* had a rough few days, and I *know* that this probably isn't a good idea. But then, I've known that all year about a variety of things, and where exactly has that got me? At least this bad idea feels pretty good right now—don't you think?'

Rhys's gaze was locked on hers, and it didn't move as he nodded slowly. Oh, so slowly. As if he really didn't want to but was helpless to do otherwise.

The idea that such a strong man could feel that way because of *her* was the most delicious sensation.

'I'm still a reclusive widower who doesn't like Christmas, Ana,' he said, 'I'm not going to be your Prince.'

Ana laughed out loud. 'A prince is the last thing I want, Rhys,' she said. 'Tonight I don't even want to be a princess.'

At some point they'd moved even closer together. Close enough that it would be so easy to reach out and—

'Do you realise you've never touched me?' Ana said. 'It's been driving me crazy. I—'

'Yes,' Rhys said hoarsely, and suddenly his hands were at her hips. His big hands gripped her, his fingers enveloping her waist.

For long, long moments all Ana could do was bask in the sensation of Rhys's hands against her body. Even through the cotton of her T-shirt and the denim of her jeans his touch was electrifying. All she could think about was the heat of his hands and the way his touch made her insides go liquid in response.

But Rhys's hands didn't move. She looked down at the way his thumbs curved at her hips, but they remained frustratingly still.

Ana's gaze returned to his. 'Rhys…?'

The way he was looking at her was *everything*. All need and want and like nothing she'd ever experienced.

'Are you sure?' he asked.

She'd barely mouthed the word 'yes' when his mouth covered hers.

His lips were firm and sure—there was not a shred of doubt in his kiss. And there was not a shred of doubt in Ana's response. Immediately she slid her hands up across his shoulders to tangle in his thick hair and pull him even closer. She slanted her mouth as he tasted her lips, tasting his in return, exploring the shape and touch of his mouth.

It was probably only moments later, but when Rhys's tongue brushed along her bottom lip she sighed in relief, and with need, as if she'd waited for ever to deepen this kiss.

She *needed* to deepen this kiss. She needed to be as close to Rhys North as she could be.

Maybe he felt the same, because his big hands had shifted at her waist to tangle in the fabric of her shirt, to slip under it and against her skin. He explored no further than her waist, the small of her back, and it was not enough for Ana. Not nearly enough.

As they kissed, their tongues tasting and tangling and exploring, Ana's hands moved from his hair to his shoulders, and then—more boldly—slid down his back to scrape her nails gently down the valley of his spine.

He liked that, groaning his approval into her mouth—and Ana really liked that response, smiling against his lips.

Rhys smiled back, and they stood like that momentarily, perfectly still but for the mingling of their smiles and their breathing. Then Ana slowly slid her hands around his waist to slide beneath his T-shirt. As her breath grew heavier, she paused at his belt for long, tempting seconds before she explored upwards, her fingers luxuriating in the heat and smoothness of his skin and the gorgeous, masculine, hard abdominal muscles beneath her fingertips.

She'd made it up to his pectorals when he stepped backwards. But before she could protest he'd whipped his shirt off over his head.

Oh. This was better. *Amazing,* as she'd said earlier—how could it have been only today? She'd said it about the view, but really it had been about him, and that opinion was only enhanced now she had his entire chest available for her perusal.

Not that she got long, as seconds later she was in his arms again and he'd lifted her effortlessly—making her feel light and tiny for the first time in her life—and she was sitting on the granite counter, the cheese platter shoved far out of the way.

He stood between her legs, kissing her again, no longer exploratory or playful. It was as if they'd sized each other up and this was *serious* now. This was proper, intense, all-consuming kissing—kissing that made it impossible for her to think of anything but him. His lips on her and his hands on her body. His hands beneath her shirt, shoving her bra up and out of the way, all heat and want and need…

And it was *glorious.* It was what she wanted. *He* was all she wanted.

He wasn't her Prince and she wasn't his Princess.

But they were what each other needed.

Just for tonight.

CHAPTER SEVEN

IT WAS DARK when Rhys woke.

He lay in Ana's bed.

Why had they chosen *her* bed? He couldn't remember—much of the night had been a blur. A *good* blur, though. An unexpected blur.

Unexpected?

No. No point lying to himself now. From the moment Princess Ana had arrived at his house the air had crackled between them. He and Ana had chemistry—there was no doubting that.

Last night had felt inevitable. Where he and Ana had always been heading.

He stared up at the ceiling. So, it had happened. He'd slept with a woman after Jess.

No matter how inevitable sleeping with Ana might have felt—how *right* it had felt at the time and how right it *still* felt, actually—this was still a big deal.

Ana shifted beside him. Rhys rolled onto his side to watch her sleep.

In their haste they'd left a light on in the kitchen, and enough light spilled down the hallway to illuminate Ana's shape beneath the sheet. Her hair fanned out across the pillow and her hands lay haphazardly on the mattress between them.

She was beautiful.

He liked her.

Oh.

Something inside him shifted. His subconscious appeared comfortable with admiring her beauty, but not so much her personality.

For the first time, he felt uncomfortable lying in Ana's bed. Suddenly lying here felt…*disloyal.*

Which he knew, objectively, was ridiculous.

Even more ridiculous given that he'd had opportunities to sleep with attractive women before but had felt he wanted more. He'd wanted a connection. He'd wanted something *real.*

Now he'd had it. Now he'd had an amazing night with a gorgeous woman whom he liked…

He realised he really needed to get out of her bed.

He sat up and swung his legs over the side of the mattress.

Ana's hand was suddenly at the small of his back, her nails skimming lightly across his skin.

Rhys looked over his shoulder. She was still sleepy, her lids heavy.

'Rhys?' she said.

'Your Highness?' he responded.

It was a deliberate decision not to say her name, and one he immediately regretted as he watched Ana's eyes widen and then hurt flicker in her gaze.

But she instantly understood.

Her hand fell away from his body and she tangled her fingers in the sheets, tugging them up higher. Hiding herself from his view.

Casually, she snuggled back into her pillow. Then, as she rolled so that her back was facing him, and so he could no longer see her face, she spoke.

'Goodnight, Mr North,' she said. Very calmly, very politely. Regally, even.

'Goodnight, Your Highness,' Rhys said.

Then he left.

Ana decided to make herself toast for breakfast the next morning.

It was early. *Really* early, actually. But it had been impossible for her to sleep once she'd realised what she had to do: go home to Vela Ada.

Her little escape to Italy was over.

Ana stood on her tiptoes as she reached for a jar of peanut butter in the pantry. Rhys clearly wasn't a fan of the spread, as it was stashed away amongst dusty spice jars and miscellanea on a high shelf.

As she grabbed it, her hand brushed against a glass vase stored beside it and the oval-shaped vessel wobbled alarmingly. Peanut butter forgotten, Ana grabbed for the vase—thankfully catching it, but in the same movement knocking a shoebox from the shelf and onto the floor.

Letters—unopened letters—spilled from the box and across Ana's feet.

Quickly she dropped to a crouch, gathering up the letters—and the occasional postcard—and placing them back in the box.

She didn't *mean* to look at them, but it was impossible not to notice that nearly all the stamps were Australian and nearly all the senders had the surname North. She'd guess that most of the envelopes contained cards or invitations—the shadow of Christmas- or birthday-related artwork was visible through some of the envelopes, while at least two were clearly expensive formal wedding invitations. But a few were definitely letters.

Ana hadn't realised people sent so many actual letters these days.

But not one had been opened.

Ana turned over the very last postcard in her hand before she placed it back in the box—it was a birth announcement, with a black-and-white photograph of a baby on one side, and a scrawled message on the other.

Before she could read past the date—more than two years ago—Ana stuffed it into the shoebox, shoved on the lid and put the box back exactly where she'd found it.

Rhys's mail was absolutely none of her business. *None.*

This time she retrieved the peanut butter without issue and a few minutes later was standing at the granite counter—which she'd cleared of all the cheese they'd forgotten about last night—and making herself focus on eating her toast rather than wondering why Rhys was hoarding unread mail.

She was starving, actually. She and Rhys had skipped dinner last night, after all.

The reason for the forgotten cheese and missing dinner made her lips curve into a smile and very effectively distracted her from her accidental shoebox discovery.

Last night had been good.

Great, actually.

Amazing, really.

Unlike anything she'd ever experienced.

If she'd had any lingering doubts about her decision literally to flee from Petar as fast as her wedding heels could carry her, they had been blasted away now.

Last night was what she wanted in her happy-ever-after. That all-encompassing desire, that passion, that *connection*.

Like an idiot, she hadn't even slept with Petar, having some misguided idea that she was being old-fashioned and romantic.

How crazy was *that*? She wasn't a virgin, but in her crazy princess year she'd attempted to reinvent herself in so many different ways. Waiting for marriage had seemed a sensible idea. It was as if 'Princess Ana' was a character she'd been playing.

Well… She'd been Ana Tomasich last night. All weekend, actually. From the moment she'd dropped that bouquet.

'Good morning,' Rhys said as he walked into the kitchen.

He ran a hand through his hair as he blinked

at her with sleepy eyes, and in T-shirt and low-slung tracksuit pants he still managed to look unbelievably sexy.

'Good morning, Rhys,' Ana said.

No more of this formal name nonsense. They'd both made their point last night, when Rhys had gone back to his own bed. They'd formally put distance between each other.

Well, Rhys had put distance between them and she'd gone along with it. Although she would've done the same thing. Eventually.

Because putting distance between them was the only thing to do. Last night had been great in so many ways, but it wasn't as if it was going to happen again.

It wasn't as if they were going to start *dating* or anything. How would that even *work*? A princess and a Castelrotto recluse?

They lived in different countries. She was a princess and Rhys was still grieving his wife's death. And she'd almost married the wrong man. The *last* thing she wanted was to leap into another relationship.

So, yes. She was glad Rhys had returned to his own bed.

As she watched, Rhys reached for a coffee

mug from an overhead cupboard. The casual, unremarkable action drew Ana's attention to the heavy muscles of his shoulders and arms, and the sliver of tanned skin where his T-shirt rode up ever so slightly.

Yes. She was *mostly* glad Rhys had returned to his own bed.

'I'm going home,' Ana blurted out suddenly.

She needed to be focusing on logistics, not remembering how that skin and the hard musculature beneath had felt beneath her fingertips.

'Today,' she clarified. 'It's all organised. I've already spoken to Adrian and Dino.'

Rhys turned to face her, coffee mug in hand. He met her gaze, but he was doing that *thing* he did. Where Ana couldn't work out what he was thinking.

'That's great,' Rhys said. 'I'm glad you feel ready.'

'I'm not going back to Petar,' Ana said, having no idea why she felt compelled to explain.

'I know,' he replied.

She saw *something* then. A flicker of—what? Amusement?

'You're so sure I won't go back to him after a night with *you*?' she said, her tone more tart than teasing. She hadn't meant it to sound that way.

'You were never going back to him,' Rhys said. 'You don't love him.'

Ana nodded, then managed to smile about the most significant misstep of the past twelve months. 'Yes, I suppose I forgot that love is a rather critical part of a successful marriage.'

She had managed the light tone she'd intended that time, but when Rhys replied he was utterly serious.

'Yes,' he said. 'Make sure you marry for love next time, Ana.'

For long moments that sentence hung between them.

Marry for love.

There was a knock at the door. It was time for her to leave for the airport.

Ana pushed the remainder of her toast away and walked up to Rhys. Close enough she had to tilt her chin upwards to meet that sharp blue-grey gaze.

'I will,' Ana said. 'I promise.'

Then, on tiptoes, she pressed a kiss to his cheek.

That was supposed to be that, but she found she couldn't make herself step away. Instead her lips remained a breath away from his skin—

and then, after Rhys turned his head ever so slightly, his lips.

Then, somehow, they were kissing.

Had he kissed her? Ana thought he had. But maybe not—and did it really matter?

It was a different kiss from last night. This one wasn't going anywhere. Not to a bedroom, and not to any tomorrow.

It was just a slow, thorough kiss, where they explored each other's lips and mouths and touched absolutely nowhere else. This was a kiss that was *only* about the kiss.

It was intense.

It was probably supposed to be a farewell kiss, but at some point it began to feel different. It began to feel…*intimate*.

And that was when they both stepped away. But again—like she'd wondered who'd started the kiss—Ana couldn't say who had been the first to end it.

But, equally, it didn't matter.

The kiss was over.

This was over.

'*Hvala*—thank you for this weekend, Rhys,' Ana said.

'Goodbye, Ana,' Rhys said.

Minutes later Ana was back in the car that

had brought her here only two days ago, driving away from Rhys and from Castelrotto.

And Ana knew she would never see Rhys North again.

CHAPTER EIGHT

Four weeks later

IT WAS DURING Sunday dinner at Ana's grandparents' house—a small cottage a short drive outside of Vela Ada's capital city—that Ana realised her period was late.

It was just after she'd helped her *baba* clear the plates from the main course—Baba had made *crni rižot*, squid ink risotto, and she was standing in the kitchen alone, about to arrange the *hrstule* she'd made onto a platter for them all to share.

Ana could hear her family chatting away happily in the dining room. Dino was on duty tonight and, as the Tomasichs always did on this traditional, regular Sunday night dinner, they'd invited him to join them. His deep voice mingled easily with her mother's higher-pitched, modulated tones and the softer voices of her grandparents that both crackled with age.

After a few weeks of furious media attention things had finally started to calm down for Ana. This was the first Sunday dinner she'd attended since her return, after previous attempts to leave her own home—a luxury villa, owned by the palace for centuries and located right on the water in the city of Vela Ada—had been thwarted by swarms of paparazzi.

But day by day people had lost interest in the story, especially as both Ana and Petar had declined to speak directly to the media. Ana and Petar had issued only a press release that had been scant in detail—it had simply announced the conclusion of their relationship, and said they hoped to remain friends.

Ana hadn't been keen on the 'friends' bit, as she was now convinced Petar had only ever wanted her for her title, but the palace communications secretary had been insistent.

Privately, Ana believed Petar had agreed to the press release only because he was convinced Ana would 'come to her senses.' He'd used that phrase many times, as if Ana were some rebellious teenager going through a phase rather than a woman who was finally taking control of her life. He insisted on phoning her regularly, for one-sided conversations—his side—but beyond that they had zero relationship.

This suited Ana just fine. Despite her mother's disappointment—it had only softened marginally since her wedding day, and things were still tense between them—Ana *knew* she'd done the right thing.

So today, as she'd been frying the knotted pastries she now held listlessly in her fingers, she'd been feeling rather good. She'd been feeling *normal*. As if she'd finally begun to work out this whole princess thing and realised she *could* retain herself in this new world of hers. It was up to her how she lived this life she'd never expected.

And so she'd made *hrstule*, for the first time since she'd become a princess, and actually rather enjoyed cleaning up the oil that always splashed everywhere when they were shallow fried because it had all felt so *normal*.

Except for looking at the million-dollar views from the fancy kitchen she'd barely used in the past twelve months.

But yeah. She had been being Ana Tomasich again, and it had felt really good.

But now, with those same *hrstule* in her hands, she didn't feel good at all.

She felt terrified. 'Need a hand, *bebo*?' her grandmother called out from the dining room.

'No, no!' Ana managed with a light tone. 'Just daydreaming. Won't be a moment.'

The conversation continued in the dining room as Ana swiftly piled up the pastries and dusted them with icing sugar.

She tried to do the maths in her head. Tried to remember the latest her period had ever been. Tried to work out a way that there could be anything but the most obvious conclusion.

But she came up with nothing.

She was over a week late.

There was only one thing she could do.

Take a pregnancy test.

Ana strode into the dining room with a smile but couldn't meet anyone's gaze. No one noticed—they all carried on with their happy conversations, completely oblivious.

Which was a relief. Ana needed time to process this. To know for sure. To gather her thoughts…or something.

Right now it felt as if her thoughts were riding a rollercoaster in her brain, lurching in loops and vertical drops that matched the sinking sensation in her stomach.

When she was back in her seat, her *dida* offered to top up her wine.

Ana declined with a perfect smile and then tried to remember if she'd drunk more than this half glass of wine in the past month? She didn't think so… She wasn't a big drinker, and certainly not when she was home alone. The last time she'd drunk wine had been…with Rhys.

As her wayward thoughts had taken her so many times in the past weeks, instantly she was back in Castelrotto, sharing kisses that tasted like Chianti, with the small of her back pressed against the hard edge of the kitchen bench and her breasts flattened against the hardness of Rhys.

'You okay, Ana?' her mother asked. 'You look flushed.'

'No,' Ana replied honestly. 'I feel a bit off. Is it okay if I head home?'

Five minutes later she sat in the back of the palace car, trying to work out how on earth a princess bought a pregnancy test without anybody knowing.

It took some effort, but Ana managed it.

The palace staff were absolutely discreet, but the issue was Ana didn't just not want the *pub-*

lic to know, she wanted *no one* to know. Not her family. Not the *royal* family.

Not yet.

So she wasn't going to call on the palace physician.

By her own choice, Ana didn't have a personal maid—let alone a full suite of staff like at the palace. Ana *did* have a housekeeper for a few hours each day, though, and that was how Marta became the only person in the kingdom to know Princess Ana's greatest secret.

Marta had a daughter of a similar age to Ana, so Marta purchased the test and then—just in case someone realised who Marta worked for—'dropped it off' at her daughter's place, before arriving at Ana's villa the following day for work with the concealed test.

By now it was more than twenty-four hours since Ana's epiphany, and she felt sure every muscle in her body was tense with anticipation.

So she tore open the test and literally ran for the bathroom.

She *needed* to know.

Now.

And a few minutes later, she did.

She left the test on the marble sink in her palatial bathroom and walked out on wobbly legs. All the tension that had consumed her had leaked out and she felt rubbery and useless.

Marta hovered at the door, looking awkward. She was kind, and concerned, but Ana thanked her and waved her away.

Really, it should be her mother here with her.

It was her mother she *wanted* here.

But how could she tell her mother—who had still not recovered from the scandal of Ana's wedding, only a month ago—that she was pregnant? Pregnant by a man she barely knew?

Ana fell onto her bed and cried.

At some point she fell asleep, but when she woke up she had a plan.

The sun was setting when Rhys's security system detected an approaching car.

He'd been working in his office, where he had screens set up across one wall, monitoring the perimeter of his property.

He leant back in his chair as he studied the approaching vehicle. It was a small hatchback, very nondescript. He certainly didn't recognise it.

He wasn't expecting anybody, so he could only assume it was a group of lost tourists in a hire car. It had happened once before—a group of very disorientated British tourists had been relieved to have his clear directions on how to make their way safely back to town.

Although this group would need to hurry. Flakes of snow had already begun to fall, and another heavy snowfall was expected this evening. The landscape was already cloaked in snow—it was always a white Christmas in Castelrotto—and Christmas Day was less than a week away.

The car came to a stop at the locked iron gates at the entrance to his property. He watched as the driver lowered a window to speak into the intercom. Now he could see the car held only one passenger. A woman with long curly blonde hair.

He pushed the button on his computer that activated a microphone.

'Can I help you?' he asked.

He watched as the woman jumped at his voice, and then heard her laugh through the speakers.

He knew that laugh.

Quickly he pushed buttons on his computer to toggle to the camera located above the intercom speaker.

Suddenly a familiar face filled the screen.

A familiar face with inexplicable curly blonde hair and purple-framed glasses.

'Rhys,' Princess Ana said, in her gorgeous sexy accent. 'I—'

But then she went silent. Her gaze dipped downwards.

'Ana—' he began. Although he had no idea what he'd planned to say next.

Why was she here?

He hadn't expected ever to see her again.

He'd hardly *forgotten* the night they'd shared—the number of times his brain replayed it had made that completely impossible—but it had been just that one night.

It was all they'd both wanted.

Her head jerked upwards again. She looked directly at the camera. 'Can I come in?' she said simply.

He opened the gate.

Once again Rhys met Ana at the bottom of the steps that led into his home.

She stepped out of the car in an outfit that looked nothing like anything he'd expect her to wear.

Her coat was lime green, with black and white faux fur at her neck, wrists and the bottom edge of the garment. She wore skintight white jeans, and pink winter boots with yet more faux fur— pink, this time. Over her shoulder she'd slung a large patchwork handbag, and her lips were painted a vibrant shade of melon.

She met his curious gaze.

'A disguise,' she said, by way of explanation.

But that didn't really explain anything.

He asked the obvious question. 'Why?'

'Can I explain inside?'

He nodded and waved her up the steps. Inside, she shrugged off her coat and boots, revealing a much calmer navy blue jumper.

But Ana clearly wasn't calm. She was jittery, barely standing still. Her gaze kept darting around the place, only rarely landing on him.

'Would you like a drink?' he asked.

'Not gin this time,' she said firmly. 'Do you have tea?'

A few minutes later he placed a steaming mug in front of her. She sat at his dining table, with the spectacular vista of the snow-covered Dolomite mountains revealed through the windows behind her.

To be honest, he barely noticed the landscape nowadays. He'd lived here for years, and it was easy for the mountains to fade into the background. But with Ana sitting there, even in that crazy wig she wore for whatever reason, he *did* notice their beauty. Especially now at sunset, when the mountains turned orange and pink.

It was as if when he was presented with Princess Ana's beauty he was able to appreciate all the beauty that surrounded him.

Ha! Rhys had to laugh at himself. That was almost poetic.

'It's a bit crazy, isn't it?' Ana said, misunderstanding his smile. She patted her wig with one hand. 'I bought it for a fancy dress party when I was at university. Good thing I still had it.' She removed the purple-rimmed glasses. 'Plain glass lenses,' she explained.

'But why the disguise, Ana?' Rhys prompted as he took his own seat. 'Who are you hiding from? And why are you without palace security?'

Ana shook her head. 'I'm not hiding from anyone in particular,' she said. 'Please don't worry. I wore the disguise to hide myself from the public. I didn't want anyone to know where I was going.'

'The royal jet and your security team did a brilliant job of keeping you hidden last time.'

'They did,' Ana conceded. 'Except I didn't want the palace to know this time.'

She met Rhys's gaze just briefly, before skittering away again.

She took a deep breath. 'So I put on the least princessy outfit I had, caught the ferry to Dubrovnik and then got on a commercial flight to Treviso and hired a car. My surname is relatively common, and I'm not that well-known outside of Vela Ada. My passport doesn't include my title, so no one intervened.' She shrugged. 'I was hiding in plain sight.'

Rhys had to admit her strategy had been effective. But the palace would be horrified when they discovered the security breach—a member of the royal family had apparently left the country undetected. Someone was going to be in a lot of trouble.

And she still hadn't answered his original question. *Why?*

The obvious began to dawn on him.

'You did all this to see *me*?' Rhys asked.

'Well…' Ana said. 'Yes.'

Rhys blinked. 'You could have called me first.'

He didn't know how he felt about any of this. His initial reaction when he'd recognised Ana in that hire car had definitely been positive, but he wasn't sure how he felt about being part of some complex super-secret tryst or something—if that was what this was. And if it was, why hadn't Ana run it past him?

'I didn't have your number,' Ana said simply. 'And—'

She didn't say anything more.

'Marko has my number,' Rhys said.

Ana opened her mouth.

'You didn't want him to know,' Rhys said for her.

She nodded.

'You *really* don't want anyone to know we slept together?'

'No!' Ana said, her eyes widening. 'I mean, yes—given the situation, I've not told anyone—but not because I'm *ashamed* or anything. Nothing like that.'

'So you wanted to make sure the next time it happened absolutely no one knew either?'

Ana's eyes widened. 'That's not why I'm here!' she said. 'I didn't come here to have *sex* with you!'

Well, Rhys had to admit that was disappointing.

But now his expression must be reflecting

what he was thinking. Which was: *Then why are you here?*

She sighed, then dropped her head into her hands, her tea completely forgotten.

She started fiddling with the wig, and moments later a mound of golden hair spilled across the back of one of the unoccupied dining chairs. Her own brunette hair hung in a thick ponytail over her shoulder.

'I can't do this in that stupid disguise,' she said.

'Do what?' Rhys said, and now he was concerned.

He dragged his chair closer to Anna so their knees almost bumped beneath the table.

'Do you need help? Is your ex harassing you? I always knew he was a—'

Ana shook her head. 'No…no.'

She'd grabbed her mug again, although she didn't drink. She just stared at it.

'Ana? Please tell me what's wrong.'

Finally, for the first time since she'd arrived, she fully met his gaze. She held it for an age, her hazel eyes flecked with gold and green.

Eventually, she spoke. 'I'm pregnant,' she said. 'You're the father.'

CHAPTER NINE

Rhys physically recoiled in his chair.

But that clearly wasn't enough, as then he stood and strode away from her, bumping into the kitchen bench in his haste to put distance between them.

He fell into the single armchair in the lounge, his back to her. He didn't say a word.

Ana remained where she was.

She gripped the mug in her hands. It was still hot—after all, Rhys had only just given it to her. But it felt like hours ago now.

Until she'd actually said the words to reveal her pregnancy, today hadn't felt real. Getting dressed up in this ridiculous disguise, her far-fetched plan to 'escape' Vela Ada that had worked so miraculously...

Catching the ferry, then the plane—even hiring the car and realising she would be driving with snow chains for the first time in her life, that she'd be actually *seeing* snow up close for the first time in her life...

And then seeing Rhys again. It had felt *so good* to see him. He'd felt like an anchor after she'd been lost in an ocean of shock since she'd seen the results of her pregnancy test.

Her instinct had been to hug him. To throw herself into his arms. But his body language had welcomed none of that.

He'd been standoffish from the moment he'd met her at the bottom of those steps. Just like last time. She didn't think he'd been displeased at her unexpected appearance. But he'd been wary. Now the house was completely silent.

Rhys remained in the chair.

Ana sat at the dining table.

She supposed she should give him space to absorb the news and she tried to do just that, tracing patterns on the outside of the cooling tea mug for long, silent minutes.

Outside, snow was beginning to fall steadily.

Eventually Ana couldn't take it any longer. She had to talk to Rhys. She *needed* to talk about this. She needed to know what he was thinking.

She pushed her chair back and it scraped loudly on the floorboards in the perfectly still house.

Rhys still didn't move.

Ana took a seat on the sofa adjacent to his chair. He had his head cradled in his hands.

'Rhys?' she prompted gently. 'I know what a shock this news is.'

He mumbled something Ana couldn't make out.

'Pardon?' she asked.

He slowly lifted his head. His eyes were red-rimmed.

Tears?

'I said, we had sex *once*—with a condom.'

His tone wasn't one of accusation, but even so Ana's back went up.

'I can assure you the baby's yours. I haven't had sex with anyone else in over a year.'

He shook his head. 'No. I'm not questioning you. It's just…' He swallowed. 'My wife, Jess, desperately wanted a baby. So did I. We'd been trying for a few years, but it was difficult with me being deployed regularly. We'd even started the process for IVF. We had an egg collection booked when—'

He ran his hands through his hair and fell back into the seat, his gaze now on the ceiling.

'And now, the first time I have sex after she dies—with a condom, no less—I get you pregnant?' He laughed without humour. 'I just can't believe it.'

'It doesn't seem fair,' Ana said softly.

First time? She'd had no idea. But then, why would she? She didn't know Rhys North at all.

Ana drew her legs up to hug her knees. Her own tears prickled. She was having a baby with a man who desperately wished he was having a baby with someone else.

The enormity of that realisation sat heavy on her shoulders.

All she had ever wanted for her future children was a father who adored them. It didn't matter if he wanted *her*. He just needed to want this baby.

Rhys shifted in his chair to look at her. 'I'm sorry, Ana, this must have been a shock for you too. I know neither of us planned it. I just…'

'Need some time to process the news. I understand.'

She pushed herself up off the couch. 'I'll book a hotel room in Castelrotto. I can come back tomorrow and we can talk more then.'

She liked how calm and businesslike she sounded.

'*No,*' Rhys said firmly. 'There's a storm coming. You aren't driving in this weather. Stay here.'

Ana nodded. 'Okay. I'll go to my room, then—give you some space. But before I do I just want to be really clear on something.' She met his gaze. 'I'm keeping this baby. And I'd really like you to be a part of his or her life. If you aren't prepared to do that, I need to know.'

Rhys's eyes widened. 'Of *course* I want to be a part of this baby's life. A *big* part. I'm its *father* and I intend to be a good one.'

Ana let go a breath she hadn't realised she was holding.

Rhys rushed to his feet, and suddenly he was holding both her hands in his.

'Oh, Ana, I'm sorry. I didn't even *think* about your situation, about your father...'

Ana's gaze was steady on Rhys's shoulder. He wore a dark grey T-shirt and there was a loose thread near the collar.

'That's okay,' she said.

Rhys squeezed her hands. 'Ana, honey, I *promise* I will never be like your father. I'll be there for this baby. We'll work it out. Okay?'

She looked up at him. His gaze searched hers.

'Good,' she said. 'I'm glad. That's all I expect from you, okay? Nothing more.'

Did he know what she was saying?

She didn't expect a happy-ever-after from

him. She didn't *want* one. After Petar—gosh, after what her father had done to her mother—she knew that happy-ever-afters weren't for her. *Especially* as nothing had changed from that one night together.

To want more from Rhys would be almost as bad as Petar wanting her only for her title. From now on she was back to being sensible, cynical Ana the librarian—who didn't get caught up in fantasies and who only cared about reality.

All that mattered was that this baby had a father.

And besides, Rhys was still in love with a ghost.

Palace Security called Rhys within moments of Ana leaving the room. They arrived at his gates shortly afterwards.

Rhys couldn't recall a thing he discussed with the head of security over the phone, or what he said to the two guards he set up in his guest house. They were different men from the two who'd been there last month—he did comprehend that at least.

But otherwise it was all a blank. His brain was pretty much packed full with one fact at the moment: *Ana's pregnant.*

It seemed he could grasp nothing else.

Oh... Except maybe the sharp tone of the palace's head of security when he'd asked one particular question.

'Any idea why Ana has run to you?'

'No, sir,' he'd said. 'None at all.'

He hardly felt that a man who'd allowed a princess to exit the country undetected was owed any explanation. Although he wouldn't have told Marko either if he'd been the one asking—and he imagined at some point soon he would.

This news was just his for now.

And Ana's, of course.

Their news.

Theirs.

It had been so long since he'd been part of anything: his marriage, the regiment, even his family... To suddenly be permanently, fundamentally paired with Ana... No, not even *paired*. There were *three* of them now.

After so many years of just being Rhys, just being *I* or *my* or *me*, he had suddenly become an *our*. An *us*.

Rhys walked into the kitchen to grab a bottle of wine and a glass but ended up leaving the bottle unopened when he remembered Ana couldn't drink. It didn't seem fair he could have alcohol to help him process this news when she couldn't…

The realisation sent him back to his favourite chair—a soft tan leather armchair that had a swivel base—and once again he collapsed into it, his gaze focused on the ceiling.

He didn't *want* this. He didn't want to be worrying about Ana and whether or not she could drink. He didn't want a relationship—didn't want someone else to *worry* about.

After all, he'd spent the past few years ensuring just that: he had *no one* to worry about. It was why he lived alone. It was why he didn't have guests. And it was why he never went home to see his family for Christmas. Or for any reason.

At least Ana had made it clear she didn't expect anything from him. She didn't want a romantic relationship. That was good. He couldn't have handled her wanting that from him and knowing he couldn't give her what she needed.

But there *had* to be some sort of a relationship now. Between Ana and himself. Between his *baby* and himself.

'Rhys?'

He shot to his feet at Ana's soft voice. She'd

taken only one step into the room, so she was more than five metres away from him.

'I'm so sorry to disturb you, but I heard a car arrive, and I can guess who it is, but I just wanted to know for sure—'

'Yes,' Rhys said. 'It's exactly who you think it is.'

Ana's shoulders slumped. 'Oh,' she said quietly. 'So much for my disguise. I'd hoped…'

Her words trailed off as she stared at the floor. Then she took a deep breath and straightened her shoulders.

She met Rhys's gaze. 'I really need to stop thinking that running away from being a princess will actually work.' She shrugged. 'This is just my life now. No ducking off to Italy to tell my one-night stand I'm pregnant without anyone noticing.'

Despite everything, Rhys laughed.

Ana's smile was tentative at first, but then a giggle burst out, and that made Rhys laugh louder.

Eventually they both became silent, but Ana's gaze had a hint of that cheeky sparkle again—a sparkle that he only now realised had been absent since she'd turned up in her wig and glasses.

'I know you ran away the way you did so you could tell me first,' he said quietly. 'Thank you.'

Ana closed her eyes and eventually nodded in response. When she opened her eyes again, she spoke. 'I had to,' she said. 'I had to know if you were going to be part of our baby's life before I could even *begin* to think about anything else.'

Unlike her very first night at Rhys's villa, Ana had absolutely no problems sleeping on this second visit to the Dolomites. She probably *should* have had issues falling asleep, given she still had absolutely no idea how the whole 'single mum princess' thing was going to work, or how her family—let alone the *royal* family—was going to react...

But she didn't. In fact, she had the best sleep she could remember having since Prince Goran had died.

Sharing her news with Rhys had been scary. It had been *terrifying*, really. What if he hadn't wanted anything to do with their baby?

She'd told herself he was a good guy, that he wasn't the type of man to ignore his own child—but of course she hadn't known that at all.

But Rhys hadn't let her down. And he wouldn't

let their baby down either—Ana knew that somewhere bone-deep inside her. He wouldn't do to their baby what her father had done to her.

So it probably wasn't all that surprising that she'd slept just fine.

The media, her family, the royal family... She'd have to deal with all that eventually, but at least she knew that she—and her baby— wouldn't be doing it alone.

Out in the lounge room Rhys was riding his bike on the wind trainer—a small contraption that held a standard bike in place so that Rhys could cycle like mad and not crash straight through his floor-to-ceiling windows.

He had his head down, his gaze focused firmly on the mountains in front of him. His pedalling didn't let up as Ana helped herself to toast and sat herself down at the dining table.

In fact, he rode all the way through Ana's breakfast and part way through the kettle boiling for tea.

He finally dismounted as Ana was absently dunking a teabag into a mug, her gaze firmly focused on Rhys.

She was having a baby with this man. She figured there was no point in playing coy. She needed to get to know him.

Although most likely there wasn't any need for her to note how he somehow—*remarkably*—managed to look good in head-to-toe jet-black Lycra. Not just good...*great*. All rippling shoulders and biceps and powerful thighs...

Anyway... She decided to keep her gaze firmly above his shoulders.

And if Rhys noticed her attention straying elsewhere, he revealed it only by the slightest, *slightest* hint of a grin.

Which Ana ignored.

Rhys wiped his face and neck with his towel, then ran a hand through his too-long hair so it was swept back from his face.

'Do you ride on the road too?' Ana asked—just to say something, and also in the spirit of getting to know this man she was having a baby with.

He nodded. 'Yes, when it's not snowing. Do you ride?'

'No,' Ana said. 'The roads in Vela Ada are cobblestoned and picturesque, but unfriendly for the uncoordinated. I barely manage to *walk* down the streets without tripping over.'

'Uncoordinated?' Rhys asked.

'Completely,' Ana said. 'Let's hope our baby inherits its athletic prowess from you.'

They both went completely silent after that comment. Ana had reminded them both of the reality of their situation. They really were having a baby together.

Rhys swallowed. 'So,' he said, 'what are your plans while you're here?'

Ana blinked. 'Other than heading back to Vela Ada this afternoon?'

Rhys's forehead creased. 'Why so soon?'

'Because I need to tell my mother I'm pregnant,' she said. 'And my family. The royal family. But my mother especially.'

Ana had kept too much from those who cared about her these past twelve months in her misguided quest to be the perfect Princess. She wasn't keeping her pregnancy from her mother any longer than necessary. Even if she wasn't looking forward to it.

'But I've only just learnt that you trip over your own feet,' Rhys said.

Ana raised her eyebrows.

'I thought I'd have more time to get to know the woman I'm having a baby with.'

'I want to get to know you better too,' Ana said. 'We've got this morning to talk—and maybe I can call you from Vela Ada regularly? Keep you posted on how the baby is doing? Or email you? I guess that's probably the easiest way to share images from sonograms and stuff.'

'Email?'

Rhys walked right up to Ana, close enough that she could smell his scent—sweat and deodorant and fabric softener—and he smelt *good*. Like everything he was: big, strong, solid.

'Is that how involved you think I'll be? A quick chat this morning and then an email here and there?'

Ana glared at him. 'Of course not. But the baby isn't here yet. We have time to work out access and other details.'

'You don't want me at the scans?' Rhys asked, and the question hung between them. He sounded hurt.

'I—' Ana stopped. 'I don't know,' she said honestly. 'It's my body, and I don't know you that well. This is all new to me—'

She'd never imagined Rhys standing beside her as a sonographer rubbed gel on her pregnant belly. She'd assumed he'd want to stay in Italy, that he had his business to run...

But as she imagined it now, the image was appealing. Seductive, even. A fantasy of the loving, caring partner, holding her hand...

But he wasn't that—not really. Ana gave

herself a mental shake. She needed to remain practical. She needed to keep some distance between them. She couldn't get lost in fantasy once again.

Again Rhys ran a hand through his hair. 'I'm sorry,' he said, holding her gaze. 'That wasn't fair. It is your body, and it's your pregnancy. But it's *our* baby, and I really would like to be a part of your pregnancy…as much as you feel comfortable.'

Ana nodded, turning this information over in her head. 'Okay,' she said. 'But I haven't even seen a doctor yet. I don't know when the scans happen. I'll do my best to keep you involved, and I'll think about having you there at some of the appointments.'

Something flashed across Rhys's gaze, so brief Ana almost felt she'd imagined it. But she hadn't—she had seen it: pain. Sadness, even.

Her gut felt tied up in knots as she warred against bursting out with: *Sure, come to all the appointments!* But she should be taking this slow. And not just for the sake of keeping her distance… Ana quite simply needed time to comprehend what was happening to her. She hadn't planned any of this, and she'd assumed she would have nine months to get her head around it—both the idea of having a baby, and also the idea of having Rhys in her life.

'Thank you,' Rhys said. 'That's fair. But can I ask something else of you?'

He was looking at Ana so intensely she fought against the instinct to drop her gaze, or to tangle her fingers together like she often did when she was nervous. But she didn't allow herself to. She held his gaze right back.

'Of course,' she said.

'Stay another night,' he said, his words low and strong. 'I need time to get to know you, more time to absorb this news *with* you before you disappear back to Vela Ada and your princess life.'

Instinctively Ana shook her head. 'I can't,' she said.

'Please?' Rhys said, his voice hoarse.

His gaze travelled over Ana's face, tracing the shape of her nose, her lips, her jaw. Then it dropped down lower—to her belly—and it was *so* tempting to say yes. To stay.

But she couldn't.

If she stayed here with Rhys—*alone* here with Rhys—would she be able to ignore the way she still felt so drawn to him? The fact he had become no less handsome, no less masculine, no less overwhelming to her senses in every possible way…

She couldn't. She *knew* that.

'Rhys, I'm sorry,' Ana said. 'But I think it's best if—'

'If you stay,' Rhys interrupted, 'I'll take you to the Christmas market in Castelrotto.'

Those words were so unexpected that Ana took a step backwards. 'I thought you hated Christmas,' she said, confused.

'I never said that,' he said. 'I said I avoid it. That I don't like it. That I don't like the way it reminds me of what I've lost.'

He had turned his head to look out at the mountains and Ana could only see the tension in his jaw, not whatever swirled in his eyes.

Was he thinking of his wife? Jessica? As he stood here with the almost-stranger he was about to have a baby with?

Ana swallowed in a failed attempt to loosen the sudden tightness in her throat.

Eventually Rhys looked back at Ana. 'You told me you love Christmas,' he said carefully. 'And I want our baby to love it the way I once did.'

He paused, his eyes once again falling to

Ana's still flat belly. Then looked up and caught her gaze again.

'I need just a little more time, Ana. Our worlds have been turned upside down, but I'd like to hit "pause" for just a while longer. For us to have a bit more time to absorb this *together* before we get caught up in the realities of it all. The paper-work and the logistics and how people are going to react.' He shook his head and his lips quirked upwards in a humourless smile. 'It sounds stu-pid, but I've just realised our child is going to be a prince or princess! How the heck is *that* going to work?'

Right now, Ana honestly had no idea.

'That's all coming,' Rhys continued, 'and we both know that. But, please, stay a little longer. Let's talk, let's hang out—let me take you to the market tonight.' His grin was genuine now. 'Come on,' he said, 'you *know* you really want to go.'

Ana realised she'd tangled her fingers to-gether, and deliberately separated her hands, shoved them into the pockets of her jeans.

She took a deep breath. 'Okay,' she said. 'One more night.'

Rhys's smile lit up his face. His gorgeous, handsome face.

'I hear the market is *enchanting*,' he said, echoing Ana's words from a month ago—from for ever ago.

Ana couldn't help but smile back. And as she did, she realised that, despite everything, she was very glad she was staying.

Rhys wasn't an easy man to walk away from.

No matter how stridently she told herself she should.

CHAPTER TEN

A FTER HIS SHOWER, Rhys made them both hot chocolate and he and Ana sat at opposite ends of his big L-shaped couch as they talked the morning away.

It felt weird at first—almost as if they were interviewing each other. Although, Rhys conceded to himself, it wasn't as if either of them had a choice: they had both unexpectedly obtained the role of parent-to-be—regardless of how well they answered the questions they asked each other.

Maybe that was why they slowly began to relax—with the realisation that neither of them was walking away. And also maybe because—by unspoken agreement—they weren't exactly asking hard-hitting questions, just questions about hobbies, movies, university, travel…

'Favourite dessert?' Rhys asked.

'Medenjaci,' Ana said, without hesitation. 'Although it's really a cookie, not a dessert. It's

like a honey gingerbread with cloves, nutmeg and cinnamon. I usually make it a lot this time of year, as it's so easy to cut into Christmas shapes. I made a mountain of them last year, for some of the kids in the library to decorate with royal icing.'

'You really do love Christmas?' Rhys asked, placing his now empty mug on the coffee table.

Ana grinned. 'Yes,' she said. 'I do. My mother always made a really big deal about it—which I realised as I got older was probably to make up for my father's absence. But I don't remember ever missing him at Christmas. I mean, I thought about him at other times—about the *idea* of having a father, not Prince Goran specifically—but at Christmas I never felt like I was missing out. My mother and my grandparents never allowed that to happen. The food, the baking, the decorations—Christmas was always magical when I was growing up. The best time of the year. It still is, actually. *Was*, I mean...' Ana paused. 'Last year was a bit weird, what with becoming an instant princess on Christmas Eve.'

'I would imagine that disrupted things quite a bit.'

Ana's lips quirked upwards. 'It did. I'd hoped that this year…' But then she seemed to rethink her train of thought and changed the subject. 'Your turn,' she said firmly. 'What's *your* favourite dessert?'

Rhys didn't bother to ask her what she'd been about to say—mainly because this conversation was determinedly superficial, but also because he knew what she'd been about to say.

I'd hoped that this year would be back to normal.

But it wouldn't be, because now, five days before Christmas, she was in Castelrotto with him, rather than baking *medenjaci* with her family.

'I'll stick with the Christmas theme,' Rhys said. 'It's probably un-Australian not to say that pavlova is my favourite Christmas dessert, but it isn't. My favourite is a dessert my grandmother used to make, and I'm sure my mum is still making.'

He saw Ana notice that distinction. The fact that he didn't actually know for sure if his mum still made it because he hadn't celebrated Christmas with his family—or at all—for the past five years.

But she followed his lead and didn't say anything.

'It's not even a traditional Christmas dessert—and it's definitely not Australian—but, anyway, it's called Queen of Puddings and it's incredible.'

'*Queen* of Puddings?' Ana asked. 'That sounds fancy.'

'Probably not compared to the desserts everyone sees on cooking shows nowadays,' Rhys said, 'but to ten-year-old me it was super-fancy, with its layers of custard, cake, jam and—the best bit—piles of meringue on top.'

'Yum!' Ana said. She picked up her phone from the coffee table and began typing something. 'Oh, there's heaps of recipes for it. I should give it a try one year for our baby...'

Ana's fingers went still, and her gaze darted up to meet Rhys's. Her cheeks had gone pink, as if she was embarrassed.

'I'm sorry,' she said. 'I know you don't celebrate Christmas. I'm getting a bit ahead of myself. I just thought it might be nice if our baby knows some of your family's traditions.'

Rhys met her gaze. 'Maybe our baby will have an Aussie Christmas one year and have my mum's Queen of Puddings.'

Ana frowned. 'But I thought—'

Rhys stood up and collected their empty mugs in his hands. 'I told you I want our baby to love Christmas and I meant it. I can't say that I'll love Christmas *myself* anytime soon, but I promise you I won't let my own feelings ruin the holiday. And I definitely want our baby to experience an Australian Christmas one day.'

All of that was true—although there were several not insignificant details he'd need to sort out first. Not the least being the fact he hadn't seen or spoken to his family in more than four years.

Ana nodded. He could see questions in her eyes and knew he had them in his eyes too. But Ana didn't need to know the messy details of his life—not right now, anyway.

It was all so complicated, and it was too much for today. After all, he'd learnt he was going to be a father less than twenty-four hours ago. As he kept telling Ana, they'd work the rest out later.

But as he stacked their mugs in the dishwasher, the clearest image stubbornly refused to shift from his brain: of him and Ana, and a toddler with dark brown hair, unwrapping

Christmas presents beside a pool, beneath the heat of the Australian sun.

Ana would have much preferred to leave her bodyguards at Rhys's villa rather than bring them along to the Castelrotto Christmas Market—but, given her recent 'escape' from Vela Ada, she knew there was no chance of that happening.

But they would at least be subtle in their protection of her. This certainly wasn't an official visit, so there was no need to have a hulking bodyguard on each of her shoulders. No one even knew she was in Italy—and Ana had learnt enough security lingo in the past year to know that the threat level of this market visit was extremely low.

So, as Rhys and Ana walked side by side along a narrow lane in Castelrotto at dusk, all rugged up in boots, coats, scarves and beanies pulled low, Princess Ana looked like any of the other tourists who mingled with the locals on the bustling streets.

And she felt like one too. In fact, from the moment she'd stepped out of Rhys's four-wheel drive she'd felt as if she'd walked into a scene from a Christmas card.

The village was magical—with its streets and

roofs frosted in powdery snow, and every tree draped in fairy lights. Sprigs of fir and more fairy lights decorated the eaves and balconies of the three- or four-storeyed buildings that lined each street, built close together and rendered in shades of white, cream and ochre. Small square windows dotted each wall—some framed with shutters, others framed with yet more Christmas fir, or lit by the glow of the Christmas lights that stretched from building to building high above the street.

Eventually they made their way to the market square, a large space anchored by an imposing church tower that stretched to the now dark sky. Hugging the edges of the tower and reaching around the market square were a series of matching wooden huts, each decorated with yet more fir sprigs and lit with candles and glowing lanterns. Each hut was full to overflowing with festive wares: from Christmas baubles to socks, crocheted tablecloths to sweets and carved wooden nativity scenes.

Three trumpet players played Christmas carols, low and gentle, from sheet music balanced on spindly metal stands, and crowds mingled around old wine barrels, holding steaming hot drinks in gloved hands.

And then there was the Christmas tree—huge, and tall enough to challenge the church tower for space in the clear night sky. It sparkled with hundreds of fairy lights and drew Ana like a magnet. At its base, with the scent of conifer mingling with mulled wine and gingerbread, she simply stood and looked at the market stalls that surrounded her.

'Do you like it?' Rhys asked, standing beside her.

He wore a navy blue coat with the collar flipped upwards and a jet-black beanie that didn't quite cover his too-long dark blond hair.

'It's perfect,' said Ana.

They began to explore the market stalls. At first Ana barely glanced at anything, hurriedly moving from stall to stall.

'You don't have to rush,' Rhys said. 'Take your time.'

Ana tilted her head, her gaze assessing. 'Are you sure?' she asked.

Rhys nodded firmly. 'Of course,' he said. 'I like watching you enjoy all of this.'

And he did. Ana's smile had been huge and constant since she'd stepped foot in the village, and her enthusiasm for all things Christmas was charming.

Ana's forehead creased—Rhys could tell she was unconvinced—but he ended any further discussion on the topic by picking up a carved wooden dove from a stall display and feigning intense interest.

He doubted Ana fell for his apparent sudden interest in woodworking, but she did at least continue her browsing, and even purchased a few handmade Christmas cards as they made their way through the market.

Rhys wouldn't have said he was having a *terrible* time—far from it, in fact. He hadn't been sure what to expect from this outing. He'd suggested it spontaneously, at the time desperate to find a reason for Ana to stay. And the market itself was just as anticipated: he did feel distanced from the festivities, and from the magic and joy every other person in the village seemed to be sharing.

But spending time with Ana...

It was weird, really. He'd needed Ana to remain in Italy a little longer, and it *had* been for the reasons he'd given her—to get to know her better, and to have more time to absorb such life-changing news—but he hadn't expected to *enjoy* spending time with her.

Yes, there were moments of awkwardness—

mostly when they both remembered the enormity of the journey they were about to embark upon—but mostly he just simply liked talking to Ana. He liked *her*.

Which, of course, he'd realised the last time she'd been to Castelrotto—although this time the realisation wasn't making him panic and feel pangs of guilt. Now he was very *glad* he liked Ana. He liked her a lot, actually—which was excellent news, given they were now so unexpectedly connected for at least the next eighteen years.

Ana had found a stall selling intricate crocheted tablecloths, and as he watched she ran her fingers gently along the delicate knotted threads. Her profile was lit by candles and fairy lights: her ski-slope nose, strong chin, full lips...

He liked her a lot.

He gave himself a mental shake.

Of *course* he still found her attractive. More than just attractive—beautiful. He suspected she still found *him* attractive too—he hadn't imagined the way she'd looked at him this morning after his workout.

But, honestly, this wasn't the time to be caught up in something as fleeting as attraction. He needed to be sensible—he needed to consider what they were doing.

They'd soon have a child to raise together, and right now things seemed okay between them. He wasn't going to mess that up with sex—especially given that was *all* he had to offer Ana.

After all, he'd *chosen* to live alone in a place where he knew nobody for a reason. For years now it had just been him. Alone. All he'd had to worry about was himself, at a time in his life when he was incapable of carrying the burden of worrying about anybody else.

But, as he'd promised Ana, he *would* be a good father. It was non-negotiable, so he'd have to work out how to care for someone again—to *worry* about someone again—without it spiralling into the kind of overwhelming storm that had ended his military career, and soon after any real connection with his family.

But it had been years now since he'd had a panic attack. Did that mean he was fixed?

He really hoped so.

But, regardless, he wasn't the same man he'd been before Jess died. This version of himself didn't have anything to offer a woman like Ana, even if he thought he was ready—or would *ever* be ready—to fall in love again.

This thing with Ana was never going to be a fairy tale.

He needed to remember that.

Rhys bought them *lebkuchen* from a stall, and they stood beneath the twinkling lights of the Christmas tree as they shared the soft spice biscuits.

'I used to think I'd grow out of this,' Ana said, as she shook biscuit crumbs from her gloves. 'You know…those bubbles of anticipation in your stomach in the lead-up to Christmas. I thought there was a deadline for when you had to be an adult, more circumspect and *mature*, or something, but it's never happened for me. I still wake up on Christmas Day and it feels special and different to me. Like no other day of the year.' She tilted her chin upwards to meet his gaze. 'Thank you for bringing me here,' she said, 'even though I know it must be difficult for you.'

Rhys shook his head. 'It's not,' he said firmly. 'At least not like you think. Being here doesn't make me feel sad. It's more…' He struggled to find the words to articulate what he meant. 'I accidentally came to the market the first year I lived in Castelrotto. I'd headed down to the village to go shopping for groceries, and the market was on. It was just like this—all perfectly Christmassy and objectively magical. But I didn't *feel* any of it. It was just lights and lanterns and a giant fir tree—it didn't feel like *Christmas* to me. It didn't feel like any of the Christmases that had come before. And it still doesn't.'

He tried to smile at Ana, but couldn't—and he realised maybe he hadn't convinced either Ana or himself that it wasn't grief that had replaced the Christmas joy that had once been so familiar to him.

Ana reached out and her gloved hand briefly brushed against his, as if she was going to take his hand in hers. But an instant later her hands were shoved in the pockets of her coat.

'Did Jess love Christmas?' she asked softly.

'Yes,' Rhys said roughly.

Nearby, the trumpets began a new Christmas carol.

'She would have loved this place.'

He still couldn't grasp the possibility of celebrating Christmas without her. Even now, with Ana and their baby, it seemed impossible—no matter what he'd said to Ana before. In fact, *all* of this seemed impossible: standing here with a princess he barely knew who was carrying his baby.

But now the Princess he barely knew had reached out her hand again, and this time she did grasp his hand in hers.

She squeezed his palm. Rhys stared down at their joined hands, and even through the layers of wool Ana's touch felt right. It felt *good*.

'Rhys—' she began.

But then a loud *crack* shattered the frigid night air, and all that mattered was getting Ana out of the market square as quickly as he possibly could.

It all happened so fast Ana barely had time to panic.

One moment she was holding Rhys's hand beneath that amazing Christmas tree, and the next his arm was around her and he was whisking her out of the market square...

But not at a run.

She hadn't any experience in security breaches, but she was pretty sure they involved a bit more drama than a brisk walk. Especially if that short, sharp noise had been a gunshot, as she'd immediately assumed it was.

But, equally, she was sure that Rhys was exiting the market with her for a very good reason.

Her heart was racing when they eventually came to a stop in a deserted lane, dark except for the strings of fairy lights and the glow of a single street lamp.

'Was that a gun?' she asked.

For the first time Ana noticed a skinny wire almost hidden beneath Rhys's beanie. Then he spoke in a low voice into what must be a microphone, tucked into the upturned collar of his coat.

Footsteps nearby drew Ana's attention and Marin and Edo—her bodyguards—came to a stop only a few metres away.

Rhys raised a hand, as if to keep them from approaching any closer. 'We're all good here,' he said.

The two bodyguards nodded in unison and then took a few steps backwards—effectively disappearing into the shadows.

Had they been that close all night?

Of course they had.

Ana had just been too caught up in the market—and in Rhys—to notice.

'Firecracker,' Rhys said in explanation.

'Are you sure?' Ana said. 'It definitely sounded like a gun.'

Rhys's lips twitched. 'Ana,' he said, 'I was in the Special Forces for a decade. If that had been a gunshot, I could've told you the calibre of the bullet. It wasn't a gun.' He paused. 'And if that had been a gun, we wouldn't be standing here having a chat about it. You'd be halfway back to Vela Ada by now.'

'Then why did we have to leave?'

'A camera. Maybe it was to do with the firecrackers, maybe it wasn't, but one of your guys noticed a pretty professional-looking camera set-up heading in our direction. Vloggers, probably.'

'And we don't want someone spotting Princess Ana with a man who isn't her ex-fiancé in the background of their video?'

'No,' Rhys agreed. 'I didn't think so.'

Ana closed her eyes and sighed. She'd made the mistake of forgetting who she was now, as she'd wandered through the market of Castelrotto. She'd felt normal.

But 'normal' wasn't running away from the possibility of being filmed. 'Normal' wasn't the man she was with having a hidden earpiece.

She pointed at his ear. 'What's with *that*?' she asked, her words full of frustration.

'I know enough about close personal protection that I convinced the guards to give us a bit more space than they wanted to give us tonight. This,' he said, pulling his collar back to reveal the microphone clipped there, 'is what made them agree. But also,' he added, 'if there was a threat, I'd want to know immediately. Seconds matter. It makes sense that I work *with* your guys, given my background.'

It was all very logical, but Ana didn't like it.

'Why didn't you tell me?'

'I guessed you wanted to forget who you are for tonight,' Rhys said. 'I figured the earpiece might shatter that illusion.'

He was correct.

'I *didn't* want to be a princess tonight,' Ana agreed. 'But I also didn't want to be patronised. Please don't do it again.'

Ana wrapped her arms around herself and walked a few steps further down the lane. She would've walked further, but she had no idea where she was, and if she did just walk off, she'd have two bodyguards and an ex–Special Forces soldier chasing her down.

'I'm sorry,' Rhys said, behind her. 'I won't do it again.'

Ana nodded sharply but kept her back towards him. Exasperation raced through her veins, and it wasn't just about Rhys and the bodyguards.

'Our baby will have to deal with all this too,' Ana said after a while. 'There are laws in Vela Ada about photographing young royals, but he or she will eventually become an adult and fair game. And even before then—even if we're not talking photos—our child will be an object of curiosity. No opportunity to live life unobserved. And he or she won't even get the choice I had.'

She heard Rhys take a few steps towards her, but he paused a few metres away. He remained silent. A few lonely flakes of snow had begun to fall.

'This is all my fault,' Ana said softly. 'I should never have agreed to accept a royal title bestowed on me by a man who didn't care about me. I should never have agreed to marry a man I didn't love. I should never—'

'Ana...' Rhys said, and in moments he was standing before her. 'Stop. None of this is your fault.'

Ana caught his gaze. They stood below the one lone street lamp, which provided more shadows than light. Beneath it, Rhys's face was all sharp angles and his cheeks were coated in stubble. He seemed even taller, even bigger than usual.

'I guess I didn't plan ahead,' Ana continued. 'Although maybe that's why I got engaged to Petar? There was a man who *wanted* all that I was so unsure about. Who wanted to be royal— who wanted the profile and the fame. Maybe I thought it would rub off on me?' She sighed. 'But it hasn't. And now I've dragged *you* into it. I've dragged our baby into it.'

At some point Ana's attention had drifted away from Rhys, and she found herself studying her boots as she shuffled them in the light coating of snow.

'Ana—'

'*Don't* get started again on how privileged I am, Rhys. I—'

Suddenly Rhys was holding both her hands in his.

'Ana, *stop*. Please. This *isn't* your fault. Neither of us planned any of this. And I certainly don't *blame* you.'

'You can blame me for the royal title our child will have. The scrutiny you'll be under from the moment people find out I'm pregnant. If I'd only said no and stayed plain old Ana Toma-sich, then—'

'Then I wouldn't have met you, Ana,' Rhys said, squeezing her hands.

Something in his tone made Ana's gaze shoot upwards, tangle with his.

'I wouldn't have met you because you wouldn't have been a princess fleeing from a media storm.'

He swallowed. The way he was looking at her was intense, like nothing she'd ever experienced.

'And I'm *glad* I met you, Ana,' he said. 'Very glad.'

They stood like that, alone together in the narrow lane, with Christmas lights twinkling above them, for long, long moments.

'I'm glad I met *you*, Rhys North,' Ana found herself saying, and realised as the words hung in the cold air that they were absolutely true. Despite what she knew lay ahead, and how much harder things were about to become.

'We're in this together now,' Rhys said. 'No more talk about blame or regret. This is *our* baby.'

Suddenly it was obvious what Ana had to ask Rhys. As obvious as if the words had been formed in fairy lights.

'Would you like to come to Vela Ada with me tomorrow?'

He didn't blink. He didn't look surprised for even a millisecond.

'I was *always* going to Vela Ada tomorrow,' Rhys said. 'I've already booked my flight. I wanted to be there if you needed me. I didn't say anything as I didn't want you to feel crowded—and I didn't want to get in your way.'

It took Ana a while to comprehend what he was saying—it was so unexpected.

'But I'd much rather travel with you,' he continued.

They were still holding hands, and Ana felt the heat of Rhys even through the dual layers of wool. Now it was her turn to squeeze his hands.

'I have to admit the royal jet is much nicer than flying commercial,' Ana said frankly.

And that made Rhys laugh, and then Ana laughed too.

At some point their hands fell apart.

But something had changed between them.

Rhys's words echoed in Ana's brain as they walked back to the car with her forgotten bodyguards trailing behind.

We're in this together now.

CHAPTER ELEVEN

VELA ADA INTERNATIONAL AIRPORT was tiny.

In all the years Rhys had known Prince Marko, he'd never actually made it to the small island nation, so he studied his surroundings as they disembarked the plane with interest.

It was cold on the Tarmac, although—as Ana had told him—it rarely snowed in Vela Ada, so the tree-covered hills that surrounded the airport weren't dusted in white. They'd landed at the private royal terminal, even though the main terminal a short distance away was hardly bustling. Ana had explained that only limited flights flew direct to Vela Ada, with the majority of long-haul flights landing in nearby Dubrovnik and visitors then ferried to the island.

But other than sharing that piece of information, Ana had been quiet all morning.

She'd barely said a word last night either, after they'd left the market—although he'd been quiet then too. But that silence had been comfortable—as if they'd reached a shared understanding. This morning something felt different between them. Ana was distant.

'I'd like to tell my mother by myself,' Ana said as they approached the royal terminal building. 'If that's okay?'

Rhys nodded. 'Of course,' he said.

The point of his being here was to…well, to *be* here. He'd had no particular plan when he'd booked his flight other than wanting to be in Vela Ada should Ana need him.

He couldn't say he knew what her 'needing him' even looked like. But he definitely didn't want to be a flight away—or even a day away, given the time it took to travel from Castelrotto to Dubrovnik without the benefit of a private jet—if she did.

He knew Ana had been surprised he'd already planned to travel to Vela Ada. Hell, she'd been surprised he wanted to attend her pregnancy scans. But she couldn't have been any more surprised than *he* was.

For a man who'd spent so many years mostly alone amongst the mountains, it was strange to feel so compelled to be close to Ana.

No—not Ana. To their baby.

He'd tried not to analyse it too much—if he

did, he got caught up in memories of Jess, and the talks they'd had when they'd dreamed of their own baby. Because was that where this came from? He'd spent so long wanting a baby with Jess, and now he was having a baby so unexpectedly he wasn't able to let it—and therefore Ana—out of his sight?

But that was the thing. If he was honest with himself, it *wasn't* just about their baby. There was something about *Ana*.

He'd meant it last night when he'd told her he was glad he'd met her. That he didn't regret *any* of this. Even as messy and confusing as it was, and as obvious as it was that his life was about to change for ever.

He couldn't regret that night he'd had with Ana. A night that had once again filled his dreams, the memories only intensified by the proximity of Ana only metres away in his guest room.

He could try to justify to himself that being in Vela Ada was purely about the baby, and that was a big part of it, no question, but as he watched Ana walk beside him now, her stride determined and—dared he even think it?—*regal*, her expression revealing nothing, even though he knew exactly how much doubt swirled in her brain, well…

He was here because of Ana too.

Ana stepped through automated glass doors and into the terminal building, with Rhys only a step behind her. From here they were due to be collected in separate cars—Ana to head to her home, and Rhys to a hotel. He was unsure what Ana's plans were—he suspected, like himself, she wasn't planning too far ahead at the moment.

But the instant they entered the marble-tiled building it was clear things were not going to go to plan.

'Ana!' a woman yelled out, followed by a string of Slavic that Rhys didn't understand.

The woman came running across the nearly empty space, her heels clicking on the tiles. Close behind her—walking briskly—was Prince Marko. Beside him was the heavily pregnant Princess Jasmine.

'Majka—' Ana began, and as the woman came closer it was obvious who she was.

Even with her silver-streaked hair, the woman was undeniably Ana's mother, with the same angular jaw and cheekbones, and a tenacity that she'd clearly passed on to her daughter.

Rhys might not speak Slavic, but he could paraphrase exactly what Ana's mother was asking. *Where the hell have you been?*

Ana was absolutely not ready to face her mother.

Yes, the whole reason for her wanting to get back to Vela Ada quickly was so she could *talk* to her mother—but it wasn't supposed to be *here*. Straight off the plane and out of sorts after spending two days alone with Rhys.

On the plane she'd kept telling herself she'd be fine once she was back at her own place and had had a few hours to herself to get her thoughts in order. After last night's revelation—that she couldn't regret meeting Rhys—and then having the *most* vivid dreams of her life, of memories created in the very bed she'd been sleeping in, she could barely look at Rhys without blushing.

So she really *wasn't* in the ideal headspace to have a significant conversation with her mother.

'How *could* you just disappear like that?' her mother asked. 'Without a word? I was so worried! Palace Security wouldn't even tell me where you *were*. Why would they do that? *Why*, Ana?'

Her mother directed an accusing glare at Rhys, who had stepped closer to her. Close enough that they looked kind of like a couple—which probably wasn't helping the situation.

Ana took a step away and immediately regretted it. There was something about having tall, broad Rhys by her side that made her feel better about everything.

But she wasn't going to step back again now. They *weren't* a couple.

Prince Marko and Princess Jasmine came to a stop beside Ana's mother. Even dressed casually in jeans, the couple looked as polished as always. Jas had confided in Ana that she had also found the transition to Princess difficult, but Ana honestly found that hard to believe. Jas was the darling of Vela Ada—while Ana had managed to embarrass the royal family once already as a runaway bride, and was about to do it again with her pregnancy.

'Vesna...' Prince Marko began, addressing her mother in a low and soothing tone. 'How about we all go back to the palace to discuss this?'

Ana had known her entire life that she was actually Marko's cousin, but it hadn't made her any less starstruck when she'd first met him and King Lukas twelve months ago. They might be blood relatives, but she'd grown up seeing the

Prince and the King as celebrities she'd read about in newspapers, magazines or on social media.

She'd even watched the televised wedding of Marko to Princess Jasmine only a few months before Prince Goran had died, and had oohed and aahed over Jasmine's dress, not to mention the whole fairy tale of Jasmine's transition from bodyguard to princess.

But at no point had she imagined she would one day be part of that glossy, photographed, televised world.

Ana's mother was having nothing of Marko's attempts to calm her.

'Ne razumijem!' she continued, meeting Ana's gaze—*I don't understand. 'Ne razumijem,'* she repeated, but more softly this time. Sadly.

Ana noticed the red rims round her mother's eyes and the dark shadows beneath them. Seeing the worry she'd caused her mother made her feel ill. Vesna had been informed she was safe, but nothing more…simply because Ana hadn't had any idea what she could say.

She should have done better.

Ana shook her head, feeling completely helpless. She couldn't tell her mother—not here. Not in front of Marko and Jasmine, and Marko's valet, Ivan, and the not insignificant number of palace bodyguards who hovered nearby.

Vesna directed her attention to Rhys, as if suddenly realising *he* might be the oracle capable of answering her questions. 'Who are *you*?' she asked.

As Ana watched, something shifted in her mother's expression. Her mother glanced back to Ana. Then back to Rhys.

'My name is Rhys North, Ms Tomasich,' Rhys answered, in his lovely strong, husky voice. 'If that was what you were asking. I'm sorry, but I don't speak—'

Vesna held up a hand to silence Rhys. Her attention was now entirely on Ana.

'Who *is* this man to you, Ana?' she asked. 'Is *he* the reason you *humiliated* your fiancé? Is *he* the man you ran to in front of *all* Vela Ada?'

'No, Mother, it's nothing like that,' Ana said. 'He—'

'I'm not stupid, *moja kćer*. I know what I can see with my own eyes.' She turned to face Rhys and began to speak in English. '*You* stole Ana from a very good man. *You* stole her from the life she *deserves*. Do you have *any* idea what has been written and said about Ana? What people

think of her after what she did? And she is none
of the things they say! *None.*'

She stepped closer to Rhys, who was so tall
that Vesna had to tilt her head up to meet his
gaze. Ana wrapped her fingers gently around
her mother's wrist and attempted to tug her
away.

'Majka,' Ana pleaded. 'Stop this—'

But Vesna shook Ana's touch away. 'My
daughter is a *princess*. She is *perfect*. She had
the life she deserved stolen from her, and when
she finally had it *you ruined it*. How *could* you?'

Tears slid down her mother's cheeks and
Vesna angrily swiped them away.

'Majka,' Ana repeated. '*Please.* Stop. Rhys
hasn't ruined anything. He's *helped* me.'

'Is *that* what they call it now?' Vesna asked,
with a humourless smile.

Rhys had remained absolutely silent throughout Ana's mother's tirade. He hadn't flinched,
hadn't moved. But now, suddenly, he spoke.
'Ana is much more than a princess,' he said.

'And I'm *not* perfect, Mother,' Ana added. 'I
never was, and I'm not now.'

Ana felt Rhys's gaze on her and realised he
knew exactly what she was about to say. It
wasn't the right place, and it wasn't the right

time. But then nothing about her and Rhys and this baby had worked out the way she'd planned, had it?

'I'm pregnant, Majka,' Ana said. 'Rhys is the father.'

Princess Jasmine gasped just as Vesna's legs gave way. But Rhys caught her mother well before she hit the floor.

Two palace cars had come to the airport to collect them.

Fortunately Vesna hadn't actually fainted—her legs had simply become wobbly at Ana's news. Unsurprisingly, Vesna hadn't appreciated being caught by Rhys, and had disentangled herself within seconds. Still, Marko had organised for the royal physician to meet them at the palace to check Vesna—and Ana—over.

But Ana hadn't even given Rhys the option to travel with her.

'I *really* need to talk to my mother,' she'd explained as they'd walked behind the very gallant Marko, who had assisted Vesna to one of the cars. 'You can go with the Prince and Princess.'

Rhys couldn't work out if he was pleased or unhappy with this. A big part of him thought it was important for Ana to have some time and space alone with her mother—who, despite her anger in the royal terminal, clearly loved her daughter very much—but another part of him was reluctant to leave her side.

We're in this together now.

Was he taking his words last night a little too literally? After all, they'd be parenting from different *countries*. Travelling in different cars was nothing.

Once seated in the car, Rhys attempted to admire the surrounding Vela Ada countryside as the two sleek cars nosed their way towards the palace: the lush rolling hills, covered in rows of grapevines or fruit trees, or densely packed with towering firs. The red-roofed villages tucked into leas and valleys. And, as they approached the capital city, the beautiful beaches and rolling waves of the Adriatic Sea.

Princess Jasmine had attempted to provide some touristy running commentary as the car wound its way through the narrow roads to their destination, but at some point she'd seemed to realise that Rhys wasn't exactly fully engaged.

Was that my plan? he asked himself. *To parent from Northern Italy?*

If he was absolutely honest, he had gone to great lengths not to consider the logistics of this baby in the past forty-eight hours and had instead stuck to the rather vague statements of *'being there'* or *'being a great father.'*

But what did that actually *mean*?

As he stared out through the darkly tinted windows at the unfamiliar landscape, at the pretty capital city…and then, most tellingly, at Palace Vela Ada, perched at the highest point of the island, it became blindingly, patently obvious that he needed to work that out quick smart.

Because as the palace gates opened and the cars followed the curved driveway towards the elaborate tiered steps at the palace entrance, it was more obvious than ever that Rhys's life had changed for ever.

And, more important—as Ana had made clear in that deserted Castelrotto street beneath the Christmas lights—their baby would be born into a life of intense scrutiny and expectation. A life that neither he nor Ana had much experience in.

Could he *'be there'* from Castelrotto?

To a man fortunate enough to have been raised by wonderful parents, with a father who had been a huge part of his life—from coaching his primary school footy team to supporting Rhys in his chosen career, despite his own philosophical objections to war—the answer was obvious.

But was he ready to leave Castelrotto? Was he ready to let go of the isolation he'd deliberately created these past few years?

Palace attendants opened his door, and he exited the car only moments after Ana exited hers—parked just in front of him.

Did she sense him watching?

As if something had made her look over her shoulder, she turned and caught his gaze.

He didn't say a word, but she nodded at his unspoken question: *You okay?* Then she returned to assisting her mother out of the car and Rhys watched, relieved, as Vesna gripped Ana's hand tightly in hers—and didn't let go as they ascended the steps.

Rhys shook his head and silently laughed at himself. As he'd realised the day Ana had told him of her pregnancy, he wasn't an *I* now—he was an *us*. Even if he remained in Castelrotto, he'd never get to be alone again in the way he'd craved five years ago.

The way he'd still needed to be only *three days ago*.

And, to be honest, the idea of letting go of that isolation was damn frightening. To so obviously embrace his responsibilities, with all the worry and fear and risk of losing it all again… To risk losing himself in all of that again…

A part of him wanted to get back into the car and be driven straight back to the airport. A *big* part of him.

But that wasn't an option any more. It couldn't be.

So instead he jogged up the palace steps to catch up with Ana.

While Ana and her mother met with the physician in one of the palace's salons, Prince Marko invited Rhys for a drink in a large circular room located at the base of one of the palace's four stone turrets.

'Welcome to the Knights' Hall!' Marko said jovially as he gestured for Rhys to enter before him.

But a moment after Marko had shut the room's door Rhys found himself shoved up against the wall, Marko's hands gripping his shoulders with intent.

'What the *hell*, Rhys?' Marko said, his words low and harsh. 'You thought it was a good idea to sleep with my cousin on the day she was supposed to marry someone else?'

'It was the day after,' Rhys clarified, unwisely, and Marko just shoved him harder—hard enough that his head whacked against unyielding stone.

It stung, but Rhys didn't make any effort to extricate himself. He was about the same size and weight as Marko, and they were both military-trained, but Rhys still reckoned he'd have the edge on the Prince if it came down to it.

But he didn't want to fight his old friend.

'Mate,' he said, 'I didn't take advantage of Ana, I swear. I'd never take advantage of any woman—surely you know that?'

The grip on his shoulders loosened, but Marko didn't let him go. The Prince shook his head. 'You might not have taken advantage of her, but you didn't do what was *right* for her.'

At this, Rhys had to grin. 'Marko,' he said, 'I think Ana is better placed to determine what is right for her than you or me, don't you think?'

Marko frowned, but his hands fell away. The Prince put a few steps of distance between them, and Rhys rubbed absently at the spot where his head had hit stone.

'We had one night together that was right for us *both* at the time,' Rhys said carefully.

He hadn't told Marko of his years of celibacy, but his friend *did* know he'd been single since Jess died.

'It's none of your business, but we used protection—and I don't appreciate your commentary on whether or not that night should've happened. That night was between Ana and me only.'

Marko sighed. 'Fair point,' he acknowledged, although he didn't seem particularly happy about it. 'You said "one night",' he added. 'I know she hasn't seen you since—although it appears Palace Security can lose a princess, I'd like to think they'd notice if she was seeing somebody—so you aren't in a relationship?'

'No,' Rhys said firmly. 'We're not.'

'You're not?' Marko prompted. 'Or you *weren't*?'

Rhys narrowed his eyes. 'We're not in a relationship.'

The Knights' Hall was furnished with several brocade armchairs, many oil paintings and a suit of armour beside the low cabinet that Marko now strode towards. From it he extracted a bottle of something that looked like Scotch, and poured only himself a drink.

As if he needed any further evidence that Marko was unhappy with him.

'This is complicated,' Marko said.

Rhys stepped away from the wall, then poured himself his own drink. He took a sip, barely tasting the surely heinously expensive liquid. 'It's my complication.'

'And Ana's,' Marko said. 'And therefore mine.'

Rhys raised an eyebrow. 'Since when do *you* care about protecting the royal family's reputation?'

Marko's past was scandalous—until his engagement to Jasmine he'd been known worldwide as Europe's 'Playboy Prince.' He'd eschewed everything about royalty—particularly when it came to anything close to royal duty.

'This has nothing to do with protecting the royal family. This has to do with protecting *Ana*. The media will tear her apart when this gets out. The timing is unfortunate, and you're not even *together*.' Marko took another long sip of his drink, then shot Rhys a sharp look. 'Why *aren't* you together, anyway? Ana is fantastic.'

The Prince was behaving exactly like a protective older brother.

'I know that,' Rhys said. 'But we just had one night. It wasn't supposed to be more.'

'So it *could* be?'

'No.'

Marko ran a hand through his hair. 'It would be much easier if you were in a relationship. When we eventually speak to Palace Communications, they're going to wish you were engaged after a whirlwind courtship.'

'I'm not marrying Rhys.'

Marko and Rhys spun around to face the now open door of the room. How long had Ana been standing there?

Ana met Rhys's gaze and her lips kicked up in a half-smile. 'I already almost married a man I didn't love and who didn't love me,' she said. 'Someone told me recently that the next time I marry it should be for love, and I'm planning on following that advice.'

Rhys tried to read Ana's gaze, but she wasn't giving anything away. Had she heard him so definitively dismissing having a relationship with her? And if she had, why did he care?

'You wouldn't have to marry him, Ana,' Marko said. 'It would just be a PR exercise.'

Ana shrugged. 'I wouldn't put Rhys through the drama of even *pretending* to be in a relationship with me. After what happened with Petar, the media attention would be unbearable.'

She hadn't moved any further into the room. Instead she just stood there, her posture perfect, her hair tied back in a no-nonsense ponytail, looking assured and in control.

'I can handle this by myself, Marko. Okay?' She met Rhys's gaze and smiled. 'I'll see you both in the dining room. Jas has invited my mother and me to stay for dinner.'

She turned to leave, but Rhys walked to her side. 'What if you didn't have to handle this yourself?' he asked, reaching out to touch her arm.

She went still, before slowly turning to face him. 'What do you mean?'

'If it helps to pretend that we're in a relationship for a while—and I imagine it will—then I'm all for it.'

Ana blinked. 'Really? *Why?*'

This close to her, Rhys realised there was a wobble to her lips and a sheen in her eyes.

'Because you didn't get pregnant by yourself. It seems unfair you're the only one who has to deal with the consequences.'

For a long moment they just stood like that, looking at each other. Rhys was sure Ana was about to say something. But finally all she managed was a brief 'Thank you', before she disappeared down the hall towards the dining room.

After she'd left, Marko cleared his throat behind Rhys.

His friend was smirking. 'Just one night?' he asked.

Rhys didn't feel that question was worthy of a response.

But as Marko walked past him, also to head for the dining room, the Prince said, clearly and calmly, 'If you hurt Princess Ana, I will destroy you.'

Rhys stayed in the Knights' Hall to finish his drink.

He didn't need Marko reminding him to be careful. The last thing he wanted was to hurt Ana.

And to make sure he didn't do that, he just needed to forget that he'd never stopped wanting her.

CHAPTER TWELVE

ANA STEPPED INTO the palace foyer well before ten a.m. the following day.

The palace attendant who had opened the doors for her had disappeared to locate the Palace Communications Secretary, whom she was about to meet with Rhys, so she was left alone in the marble-tiled expanse.

She was early—but she'd literally had nothing else to do other than think about this meeting, so she'd eventually decided she might as well stop pacing the lounge room of her villa and come to the palace.

As she waited, she admired the twin staircases before her, each sweeping up to meet at the first-floor landing. She'd always loved this space: its grandeur, its *royalness*. This, as much as the castle's turrets, was what made this place so special.

In one of the bedrooms, or the salons, you could almost forget where you were. You could convince yourself you were in a particularly fancy hotel, or something. But not here. Here in the foyer, you were undeniably in a palace.

Above her was surely the largest chandelier ever made, and before her—hugged by those glorious staircases with their rich red carpets and gilt handrails—was a Christmas tree. It filled the space with the clean, fresh scent of fir, and its colourful Christmas lights and decorations were reflected in the mirror-shine marble beneath her ankle boots.

If she was ever going to feel like a princess, it was here, standing in this foyer.

The first time she'd stood here, almost a year ago, she certainly hadn't felt like one. She certainly hadn't felt she belonged in this place.

But today, Ana realised suddenly, she *did* feel as if she belonged here. She felt as if her *family* lived here.

Although the main residents—King Lukas, Queen Petra and their son, young Prince Filip—were at the Pavlovic Estate in central Vela Ada for Christmas, she did visit them, and Prince Marko and Princess Jasmine, regularly.

She knew, deep down in her soul, that she was genuinely welcome at Palace Vela Ada.

The entire royal family had embraced her as one of them.

As part of the royal family.

Tears prickled out of nowhere, and Ana was swiping at her eyes when footsteps announced the arrival of the Palace Communications Secretary.

Ana spoke as she turned to meet her. 'I don't expect to start our meeting early—' she began, before her gaze fell on a man who was most definitely *not* the blonde-haired communications secretary Ana had been expecting.

'Rhys!' Ana said, and her stomach did that annoying somersault it insisted upon doing in his presence. She ignored that and smiled. 'Good morning! How are you?'

He grinned his gorgeous grin, which triggered yet another tummy flip.

'Let's just say I could get used to living here. My suite is almost as large as my house, and the chefs will literally make you anything you want for breakfast.'

Ana realised he'd noticed her wiping at those silly tears when he studied her carefully.

'You okay?'

She nodded briskly. 'Of course. Just being a

little sentimental. It's probably the baby hormones.'

She made that comment blithely and then immediately realised it was probably true. The physician had made her pregnancy sound *very* real last night, scheduling her in for a dating scan and providing her with booklets full of information. Not that it hadn't felt real before now...but that had been more in relation to how having a baby would change her life. Not the mechanics of what was happening to her body right this second.

'I just realised that I'm part of the royal family,' she suddenly blurted out.

Why had she told Rhys that?

She fully expected Rhys to say something smart, given how dim-witted that statement had sounded out of context. Something like: *That's usually how you end up becoming a princess, Your Highness.* But instead he said, 'I'm glad you've realised. Because you are.'

Ana had noted the tension between Marko and Rhys last night. She'd overheard only the end of their conversation—notably Rhys reiterating his lack of interest in a romantic relationship with Ana—but she'd guessed what Marko had been doing. Rhys had just confirmed it. He'd been acting like a protective older cousin.

Her warm, fuzzy feelings in relation to Marko's actions were suitably neutralised by the reminder of Rhys's declaration of wanting never, ever to be in a relationship with her, and she straightened her shoulders, shifting her smile from genuine to her much-practised princess smile.

As she'd told herself many times last night, and again this morning, it was silly even to be bothered by Rhys's words. It wasn't as if anything had changed. It wasn't as if *she* suddenly wanted to jump head first into another ill-thought-out relationship.

But still... Did he have to be *quite* so definite?

Despite her best efforts to tell herself otherwise, it had stung.

'Your Highness!'

The sound of stilettos on marble announced the arrival of the Palace Communications Secretary, Mirjana, at a brisk walk.

She was quite a short woman, with polished hair and a penchant for dark red lipstick. Ana had had quite a lot to do with her, both after Prince Goran had died and then again when she'd become a runaway bride. Mirjana determinedly put a positive spin on everything and seemed rather to enjoy all the extra work Ana had been providing her with.

Ana liked her a lot.

Mirjana grinned as she looked from Rhys to Ana and back again. Then she literally rubbed her hands together.

'Let's go create the romance of the millennium!' she announced with glee. 'Follow me.'

The palace car purred to a stop outside one of Vela Ada's finest dining establishments. Princess Ana was its only passenger.

The media weren't going to be tipped off about Ana's dinner date with a 'mysterious stranger' until shortly after Ana and Rhys had enjoyed their entrée, so Ana knew she wasn't about to step out onto the street and face the paparazzi.

No one knew she was here—yet—but still Ana's pulse raced. Fast enough that she brought her fingers to her neck, as if the insignificant pressure of her hand could slow her accelerating heart.

She took several deep breaths as she waited for her driver to open the door. She was being ridiculous. It was just *dinner.*

Her door was pulled open and Ana swung her

legs out onto the cobblestones, then looked up to thank her driver...

But it was Rhys holding out his hand to assist her.

Rhys in a midnight-blue suit, snow-white shirt and matching blue tie. Rhys with his usually just that little bit untidy hair slicked back *just* right. Like, *very* right.

Automatically she took his proffered hand, and as his skin touched hers Ana gasped. Her gaze flew up to meet his, and for just a moment they went still—Ana still seated, Rhys standing.

It was as if they needed time to absorb the electricity of their touch, to allow for all that instant heat and tummy flipping...

Although Ana supposed she could only speak for herself. Rhys probably couldn't work out why she was still sitting in the car like an idiot.

Except he hadn't exactly tugged at her hand to hurry her up. And his gaze was properly drinking her in, from her ponytail—very chic, so her hairstylist had told her—to her emerald-green boatneck dress with its cut-outs at the shoulders, her dark tights and suede heels.

Ana shivered under his perusal.

'You're cold,' he said, and pulled her to her feet.

Ana's driver materialised with her houndstooth coat, but she shook her head. She literally had metres to walk to reach the restaurant door.

Rhys didn't drop her hand as they walked towards the door. That door was also opened for them, and then they had several flights of stairs to ascend to reach the restaurant's famous rooftop location.

The whole time Rhys didn't drop her hand.

Was this part of the script?

Ana couldn't remember—but then, she could barely *think* when Rhys was touching her.

Surely they had touched over the past few days?

Yes, they had—just after she'd told him about her pregnancy. But his touch then hadn't sparked all these fireworks…which made sense, given the conversation they'd been having. And they'd held hands again at the Christmas market, but that had been through layers of woollen gloves.

Even then his touch had made her heart race, but this was a whole other level. This was exactly the way she'd felt the first time he'd touched her in his kitchen. It was all about heat and attraction and—no matter how much she didn't want to feel this way—*want*.

It was kind of awkward to walk up a staircase hand in hand, but Rhys didn't drop his touch.

Ana didn't mind. But just before they took the last few steps that would put them in view of anyone on the landing, his hand fell away.

At the top, the maître d' greeted them and immediately directed them to their table.

It wasn't a particularly large restaurant, and usually bookings were required months in advance. Consequently nearly every table was full. As they crossed the terracotta-tiled floor, several people looked up from their meals, and Ana watched as each one of them recognised her.

That was the thing about being a surprise princess and a runaway bride—she'd become rather well known.

She also watched as the diners saw Rhys, and saw their eyes widen as they put two and two together.

She knew this was exactly the point of the dinner, but still… She couldn't pretend she hadn't noticed the disapproving glances, or that they didn't sting.

Their table was located just slightly away from the other diners.

During summer, when the glass walls of the restaurant were concertinaed open, they would be greeted with a vista of red-tiled roofs, undulating down towards the Adriatic Sea. But tonight, with the sun long set, a different vista awaited Ana and Rhys.

This vista was a sparkling, twinkling one—partly because of the cast-iron lamp posts that edged the city's streets, and the many windows dotting the sandstone buildings of Vela Ada—but of course it was the city's Christmas lights that made the view truly spectacular. White and coloured lights twined between the lamp posts all the way to the marina, and more elaborate lights straddled the streets that led to City Hall. Those lights, up high above the passing cars, were formed of stars and baubles, nativity scenes and candy canes.

And right at the end—in front of City Hall—was the Christmas tree Ana had stared at through her tears from in the library, the day she'd found out she was a princess.

Even after they were seated and their wine had been poured Ana found herself gazing at that tree. This year, she noticed, the lights were different. Rather than being scattered all over the tree, this year the lights were arranged like a giant single piece of tinsel, winding its way from the glittering star down to the street below.

'Do you know,' Ana said, holding the wine she knew she wouldn't be drinking, 'it's only three days until Christmas and I keep forgetting about it? I'm not even sure what I'm doing on Christmas Day any more. Is that part of this thing?'

She meant their supposed relationship.

'We're both having Christmas dinner at the palace,' Rhys confirmed. 'And I'm hanging out with Prince Marko and Princess Jasmine for the rest of the day,' he added. 'Marko and I were actually photographed out running together this morning, which Mirjana is very pleased about. She said it supports the "old friend" narrative. Which is not surprising, given Marko and I *are* old friends.'

Ana grinned. 'She tried so hard to make it so that you and I were old friends too. She was so disappointed we'd never even been in the same country until last month.'

Ana couldn't say *she* was disappointed Mirjana hadn't got her wish of creating the fantasy that Rhys was a close friend or an old flame. She understood what Mirjana was trying to do— how she was trying to tidy around the edges of a very messy situation—but Ana really didn't want to lie. At least not to that extent. Pretending to be in a relationship was bad enough.

Although with Rhys looking as devastatingly handsome as he was tonight, it wasn't particularly difficult to pretend. In fact, it was a lot more difficult to convince herself that *any* of this was an act.

'You look beautiful, Ana,' Rhys said suddenly.

Ana's gaze had wandered to the lights amongst the rooftops, but it now shot back to meet his.

'Oh,' she said, rather awkwardly.

What was she supposed to say?

'I mean it,' Rhys said.

He was looking at her in a way that made her realise the whole sexy hand-holding thing had *not* been one-sided—although had she ever believed it was? She knew this look he had right now. This look where his eyes, even in the muted light of the restaurant, were so clearly focused on her, so clearly full of *intent*.

And then he looked away.

He shook his head. 'I shouldn't have said that,' he said. He took a long sip of his Merlot.

'Why not?'

The question had escaped before Ana had a chance to halt it. But she genuinely wanted to know. In this beautiful, romantic setting, with

Rhys, it was difficult to remember she supposedly already knew the answer.

Rhys's head jerked up. 'Pardon me?'

Ana shrugged. 'I don't think there's a rule against us saying nice things to each other.' She smiled. 'For the record, you look very *zgodan* yourself.'

Rhys's lips quirked. 'I'm going to assume that's a *good* thing.'

'Of course,' Ana said.

Her tone was light and the tension between them lessened. Or at least was paused. Or something. Enough that they could peruse the menus and hold a conversation, anyway.

But the tension certainly didn't entirely go away. But then, it never did. It never had.

Their appetiser arrived—*pogača*—and Ana immediately started tearing off pieces of the delicious tomato, anchovy and caramelised onion stuffed bread. She'd noticed her appetite had begun to change in these past few days, and she was now pretty much constantly hungry.

Their conversation drifted comfortably, eventually landing on Ana's former career.

'Why did you become a librarian?' Rhys asked her.

'Because I love libraries,' Ana said simply.

She realised she'd finished her *pogača* before Rhys had eaten even half of his.

'Libraries?' Rhys asked. 'Not books?'

'Books too,' Ana said.

Rhys pushed his plate towards Ana.

'You don't like it?' Ana asked, disbelieving.

'I do like it,' Rhys said. 'But you can have it if you'd like.'

Ana's cheeks felt warm. 'Is it that obvious?'

Rhys shrugged, then said in a low voice, to prevent anyone overhearing, 'You're growing a baby. I imagine that requires a lot of energy.'

'It appears so,' Ana said. But she shook her head. 'No, I'm fine, thank you. And the last thing we want is someone noticing me eating for two, when according to Mirjana I'm yet to conceive.'

Yet again words had escaped before Ana had a chance to censor them, and her cheeks went hot. The last thing *she* needed to be doing was reminding them both of the night they *had*, in fact, conceived.

'Books are just a part of libraries,' Ana said hurriedly, returning to their original, safer conversation topic. 'A big part, of course, but libraries are so much more. There's the obvious stuff—access to computers, the internet, and activities for kids—but for me growing up it was more about the physical space. You know... It was a place where I belonged—where *everyone* belonged. If you think about it, there aren't many places where you're welcomed like that— where you can just *be* and you don't need to explain yourself, where you don't have to rush, you don't have to know anyone.'

'You needed a place to belong?' Rhys asked.

Ana tried to explain. 'I wouldn't say I didn't belong elsewhere—I mean, I had a couple of good friends at school, and I certainly felt loved and as if I belonged at home. But I guess...'

She'd been going to say something generic, about how libraries were a conduit to the broader community and civic life, but she didn't. Instead she found herself telling him something no one else knew.

'When I was growing up, my mother was really open with me about who my father was,' Ana said. 'She had photos to show me of Prince Goran, and she talked to me a lot about him when I was very young. But as I got older, and better understood how he'd abandoned me, I didn't want my mother to talk about him. It made me angry for her and angry at him. I know my mother wanted me to be more interested—wanted me to carry on her crusade for Prince Goran to acknowledge me—but I was never going to do that. I was never going to chase after a father who didn't want me.'

Ana looked out over the rooftops again.

'But I *did* want to know more about the other half of my family. I wasn't going to use the computer at home in case my mother realised what I was doing and got the wrong idea, and I wasn't going to use the computers at school in case anyone noticed. You have to remember literally *no one* believed my mother. I didn't want to start up the gossip again, after it had taken so many years for my mother to move on from the original scandal.'

Their main meals arrived, but neither Rhys nor Ana began eating.

'So I used to go to the library after school. But I didn't use the computers there—instead I read history books about the Vela Ada royal family. From centuries ago to the present. I read about the history of Palace Vela Ada, I read about the old King Josip and Prince Goran's parents—I read anything to do with those people, and at the back of my mind I was thinking *That's my great-great-great-grandmother*, or *That's my second cousin.*'

Ana met Rhys's gaze.

'I could do that in the library and no one questioned me. I could be an anonymous schoolgirl and read anything I liked and that was okay.'

Ana realised she was tracing the tines of her fork with her fingertips, and made herself keep her hands still on her lap.

'Maybe that's why I felt I belonged at the library,' she said. 'Maybe at the library I *was* part of the royal family. I had all these relatives… cousins…a father. Everywhere else he was Prince Goran. Reading those books, in my mind, I called him my father.'

Ana found herself suddenly extremely focused on her dinner, and rapidly sliced her grilled fish into many pieces. She wasn't sure why she'd just told all that to Rhys. She supposed she would tell their child one day. So she might as well tell Rhys too.

But that didn't ring true. She always found herself sharing more of herself with Rhys than she usually did with anyone. Than she *ever* did with anyone.

'Prince Goran was mad not to want to be part of your life.'

Ana looked up from her meal to meet his gaze. She appreciated Rhys's sentiment, but she had no idea if Prince Goran had regretted his decision. He'd given no hint in his letter. Maybe he'd wished things were different, and that was why he'd finally acknowledged her birth? Or maybe he was the type of man who did the right thing—which acknowledging her paternity undoubtedly was—only if there were no negative consequences to him. And, close to his death, that was the situation he'd found himself in.

'Are you close to *your* father?' Ana asked.

Rhys took a moment to respond.

'We're very different in some ways, but he's always been a wonderful dad.'

He'd spoken carefully and hadn't really answered her question.

'Does he visit you often in Castelrotto?' she asked.

She popped a piece of fish in her mouth and ignored the twinge of jealousy as she imagined having a father who would cross the world for his child.

'No,' Rhys said flatly.

Ana swallowed. His entire demeanour had changed.

'He doesn't like to fly?' Ana prompted.

'No, nothing like that,' Rhys said. 'I haven't invited him.'

Rhys had done that shuttered thing with his eyes—packing away his emotions and becoming neutral, revealing nothing.

An uncomfortable, foreboding heaviness settled in Ana's stomach, and her voracious appetite instantly disappeared.

'Do you go back to Australia much to visit your family?' Ana asked, her words brisk.

But she had a feeling she already knew the answer. She already knew he hadn't shared Christmas with his family for many years. She already knew he had a small mountain of ignored invitations stuffed in a shoebox in his pantry.

'No,' Rhys said. 'I haven't seen any of my family for a long time.'

'But you were *close* to your family,' Ana pressed, remembering his stories of joyful Christmases past. 'Why don't you see them?'

Rhys shrugged, but it was far from convincingly nonchalant. He remained silent.

Ana tilted her head as she studied him. As she watched, Rhys drained his wine. Then he placed the glass down carefully on the white tablecloth, keeping his fingers wrapped around the stem for far longer than necessary.

He met Ana's gaze again. 'After Jess died I spent a lot of time in Melbourne. There was the funeral, of course, and then a few weeks living with my parents. But eventually I needed to go back to the barracks, which are based out of Perth—more than a three-hour flight away. I was looking forward to it, actually. I was *desperate* to go back to work. I loved my job. I loved the mateship, the teamwork of the regiment. And I needed that structure back in my life. *So* badly.'

His gaze was steady on Ana's now.

'But when I got on the plane, I had a panic attack. Almost the entire flight my mind was examining every single thing that could possibly happen to those I loved while I was away from home. Logically, I knew why I was doing it—I was deployed in Afghanistan when Jess died, so I was linking being away from home with her death. I could be as logical as I wanted, but it made no difference. For three hours or more I wasn't able to function.'

He looked away, just briefly. He closed his eyes and swallowed. Then he looked back to Ana.

'I think I hid it pretty well. I mean, I don't think anyone around me knew what was going on. But that didn't matter—*I knew*. I needed to get my anxiety under control or I'd never be the soldier I'd been for my whole career. Back at the regiment, I saw the doctor, but it was a waste of time. Nothing helped because I'd changed. I couldn't shut out the rest of the world when I was on a mission any more. I was too busy worrying about things I couldn't control—and my whole job was about being in control of the moment. So I retired.'

None of this explained why he didn't see his family, Ana thought.

'Saying goodbye to my family never got any easier,' Rhys said, answering her unspoken question. 'But I couldn't live in Melbourne. It was a place I didn't fit into any more—it was the backdrop to a life that I'd never get to experience again. So I moved to Italy.'

'And made sure you didn't ever have to say goodbye again?'

Rhys nodded. Then he cleared his throat, his gaze suddenly uncharacteristically unsure. 'I've got my anxiety under control now,' he said firmly. 'I haven't had an attack in years. I've worked out myself how to manage it—mostly by running on my treadmill until it hurts a *lot*.' His lips curved upwards. 'So you don't need to worry about it.'

'It doesn't bother me if you have issues with

anxiety,' Ana said carefully, and her gaze was steady. 'Although it *would* bother me if you avoided seeing your child because of it. It would bother me very much.'

Rhys's eyes widened. 'I would never abandon my child.'

'But it sounds like you've abandoned your family,' Ana said.

Rhys narrowed his eyes. 'I have *not* done that.'

Ana placed her cutlery down on her plate, unable to eat any more. 'You said you haven't seen your family for years,' Ana said. 'So how do you keep in touch? Phone? Email?'

She already knew that letters clearly weren't a reliable way to communicate with Rhys North.

'I haven't abandoned my family, Ana,' Rhys said firmly, and his non-answer deflated her half-hearted bubble of hope.

Her hope had been that just maybe Rhys was a terrible letter correspondent, who never saw his family but never missed a weekly video call to his mother, or something...

But, no.

'What would you call moving to another country and never seeing or talking to them again, then?'

Ana realised she'd raised her voice when

heads swivelled at a nearby table. She pasted on her princess smile until they looked away again, then leant forward in her chair.

'Rhys, I know what it feels like to be abandoned. I won't allow you to hurt our child like that. I will *not*.'

But even as she said the words she realised she had absolutely no power to prevent that. None.

She leant back in her chair and once again stared out over the city. She was utterly helpless to protect her child if Rhys wasn't capable of being the kind of father she so wanted him to be. The type of father that until tonight she hadn't really questioned he *would* be.

Deep in her heart Ana had believed Rhys was a good man. A strong man. She remembered how relieved she'd been when he'd told her he wanted to be a part of their child's life. And, like a naïve idiot, she'd simply believed him.

'Ana?'

She turned back in her chair to look at him. He still looked impossibly handsome. Perfect. Not a hair was out of place. But she wished more than anything that his jaw was rough with stubble or his hair was mussed—because *that* was the Rhys she was familiar with…*that* was the Rhys she'd thought…

She'd thought *what*?

The Rhys she'd thought she *knew*? As if she and Rhys had some sort of special connection? When she'd spent not even four days in total with this man?

Rhys hadn't changed tonight. She'd just learnt something new. Something new about a man she barely knew.

'Ana, I can't talk about this here,' Rhys said, in an urgent tone that made Ana think he'd said it more than once. 'I can explain, but not here. We're being watched, remember? We're supposed to be falling in love, not having an argument.'

Ana sighed and once again smiled her princess smile—but this time it was for Rhys.

'I understand, Rhys,' she said, *so* sweetly.

'Ana, please—'

But Ana focused all her attention on her meal, tasting nothing.

They put on a show through dessert, chatting about things that Ana forgot the second the words exited her mouth, and finally stepped out of the restaurant to the click and flash of a crowd of paparazzi. Then they fell into the cocooning luxury of the palace car.

At Ana's villa, Rhys touched her hand just before the driver opened Ana's door. Even now, electricity crackled up her arm, pooling in her traitorous belly.

She ignored it completely.

'Can I come in? We need to talk.'

Ana shook her head. 'Goodnight, Rhys.'

CHAPTER THIRTEEN

FISHING BOATS AND yachts bobbed side by side along the marina directly outside Ana's home. Her place was a traditional two-storey Dalmatian-style stone villa, with a ubiquitous red-tiled roof. Originally, it looked like the building once housed three terraced homes, with three doors equally spaced across the front, but now the entrance was through an iron gate to the side that looked very much in keeping with the centuries-old building—until you noticed the high-tech cameras and the guard waiting on the other side.

As he'd expected, Rhys was stopped at the gate while the guard contacted Ana through the security system.

'Her Highness does not wish to see you, Mr North,' the guard said.

Rhys nodded. 'Could you please let Ana know that there is at least one paparazzo photographing me right at this moment?' he said, nodding towards a woman with a very expensive-looking camera not even ten metres away from him. 'And then ask her if she would still like me to leave?'

The gate opened within moments.

The guard ushered him into a small court-yard edged with several fruit trees, all decorated with tinsel and fairy lights. Had Ana decorated them? He could just imagine it: Ana standing on a stepladder, twining the multicoloured globes amongst the glossy green leaves.

'Mr North.'

Rhys turned from the trees to see Ana stand-ing in the doorway. She wore jeans and a long-sleeved striped T-shirt, both dusted with what he was pretty sure was flour.

'Ana,' Rhys said, deliberately ignoring the way Ana's equally deliberate formality had stung.

'It's too cold to talk out here,' Ana said. 'Come inside.'

Her invitation couldn't have been any more reluctant. But he'd achieved his aim: an oppor-tunity to talk to Ana.

Ana was silent as she led him through the house. Inside, the villa was a mix of old and new, with beautiful travertine tiles, white walls and exposed original beams. A staircase led them to what was clearly the heart of the house—a large kitchen and an open living space. Up here the stone walls were left exposed on two sides, and the original windows along one side provided unimpeded views of the Adriatic Sea.

The back of the house had a modern extension, with bifold doors that led out to a deck at the rear—not that it would get much use now, in winter. It was a beautiful space, and if Ana hadn't been leaning against her kitchen bench, her arms crossed, glaring at him, he would have said so.

'I only let you in because it would ruin Mirjana's plan if I didn't.'

'I know,' Rhys said. 'Thank you.'

Ana shrugged. 'Mirjana's plan is designed to help me. I'd be crazy to sabotage it.'

Then she straightened and turned her back on Rhys as she picked up a rolling pin and began rolling out a large ball of dough.

Rhys walked closer but remained a few steps away.

'Are you making those cookies you told me about?' he asked. '*Med* something, right?'

She nodded, her attention still on the dough. '*Medenjaci*, yes.'

Rhys noticed that the oven was on, and that

a series of baking trays were already covered in various Christmas-shaped pieces of dough: Christmas trees, candy canes, stars, angels.

'I need to talk to you about last night,' Rhys said, as Ana just kept on rolling out the dough, thinner and thinner. 'I hate it that you think I'd abandon our child.'

Ana's hands went still. 'Rhys,' she said firmly, still not looking at him. 'It doesn't matter what you say now, even if you genuinely, truly believe it. I realised last night that I have absolutely no control over how good a father you're going to be. You could be the best or the worst father in the world, and I get no say in that. And last night I also discovered that you're capable of walking away from the people you love. Of *abandoning*—'

Ana's voice cracked, and she wiped angry flour-covered fingers beneath her eyes.

'I said it last night, Ana, and I'll say it again now,' Rhys said, and his voice was stronger, harsher than he'd intended.

Ana's head shot up, as if she'd only just realised he might disagree with what she was saying.

'I did *not* abandon my family, Ana. I would *never* abandon my family.' He took a deep breath. 'Five years ago I needed to find a way to cope. I needed to find a way to *exist*. I'd lost my wife, and then I'd lost my career. What you call abandonment I called coping—and, trust me, my family and friends knew exactly what I was doing. They didn't agree with it, but they understood I needed to do it. They were just glad I had purpose again—that I'd started a business, that I had some form of a life.'

Ana's hands fell away from the rolling pin and she turned to face him. But she remained silent, letting him speak.

'You know what you said before? About how you've realised you have no control over the type of dad I'll be? I can see that's frightened you, and God knows I *get* it, Ana, after the way your father treated you. And that fear of not having control? I get that too. I *so* get that. It consumed me. And being alone up in the mountains was the only thing that seemed to silence all those fears I had—that someone else I loved could be snatched away from me without warning and there was *nothing I could do to stop it.*'

Rhys realised he'd been staring out of the window as he talked, looking out at the foaming waves beneath the overcast sky.

When he looked back to Ana, she'd stepped

closer to him. Their gazes locked and Rhys *hated* the compassion in her gaze, her concern for him, her worry, her...

Wait. *Did* he hate it? Or was he having to stop himself from moving closer to her?

'I'm sorry, Rhys,' Ana said softly. 'I didn't realise—'

He shook his head. 'How could you?' he said. Then he laughed drily. 'It *does* look pretty bad. But I promise you I'm not going to hide way from my son or daughter.'

Ana's gaze flicked briefly out to the ocean and then landed back firmly on his. 'But how can you possibly *know* that, Rhys? When you've just told me that being alone is the only way you've been able to live?'

'Because something's changed,' Rhys said. 'My life isn't just about coping any more. For a long time coping was all I was capable of. But not any more.' He paused. Swallowed. 'Not since I met you.'

'No,' Ana corrected him. 'You mean since you found out you were having a baby.'

'No, since I met you,' Rhys repeated, realising it was true.

Ana's lips curved into a humourless smile. 'What's changed since you met me, Rhys?' she asked, as if she was testing him. As if she didn't believe him.

'Since I met you, Ana,' he began, his gaze unmoving from hers, 'I've wanted more than just to cope. I want to feel, I want to connect, I want to *want*. You're the only woman I've wanted in five years, Ana. You're the only thing I've wanted viscerally, deep down inside me. The only thing I've *needed*. Wanting you has changed everything.'

The green in her eyes was almost emerald in the afternoon light, and for a moment her gaze shifted into the look he still dreamed about at night. The look Ana had given him in Castelrotto, when they'd shared cheese, and Chianti, and the most amazing night together...

But then it was gone.

'How can you know that something won't happen and you'll go back to wanting to be alone, Rhys?'

He hated the worry in Ana's gaze.

'I don't,' Rhys said honestly. 'But I *do* know that I emailed two realtors before we had dinner last night. I wasn't going to tell you yet, but I've decided to move to Vela Ada. I want to be a big part of our child's life, and I can't do that from a different country.'

Rhys swallowed.

'I realise that moving here is going to involve a whole lot of goodbyes, given how much I travel for work. But I can honestly say fear didn't even cross my mind when I decided to do it. And if my anxiety becomes a problem, I'll deal with it properly this time. Not go hide on a mountain.'

'You weren't hiding, Rhys,' Ana said, and Rhys realised she'd stepped even closer. 'You were grieving.'

Rhys knew a part of him would always grieve for Jess, for what might have been. But the rest of him wanted to live *now*. He wanted to experience emotions other than fear and sadness: joy and need and passion and...love.

Rhys blinked as he digested that realisation. *Love.* Was it even possible for him to love again?

'Rhys?'

He realised Ana had said something. 'Pardon me?'

Ana was looking up at him, and even with her hair in a messy ponytail, and flour dusting her cheeks where she'd wiped away her tears, she was beautiful. So beautiful.

'I asked if you're really going to move to Vela Ada.'

He nodded sharply, his mind now on things

far more interesting than real estate. 'Yes. My business is primarily online, and my staff all work remotely, so I can work from anywhere in the world. But I was going to talk to you about it—whether I should buy in the city or countryside. I thought maybe a few acres would be good for a kid? But then, maybe being close to you would be better for school drop-offs and things like that in the future...'

Rhys didn't really know what he was saying. His gaze just kept tracing the lines of Ana's face. How had he managed not to just stare at her these past few days? This close to her, he found it impossible to think of anything but her eyes, her mouth, her lips...

'You wanted to ask my opinion?' she asked.

Was her voice lower? Breathier?

'Of course,' he said. 'Remember? We're in this together. We're an *us* now.'

'An us...?' Ana's forehead crinkled.

He stepped closer to her and balled his hands into fists to stop himself reaching out for her. 'Yes,' he said. 'It's not just me any more. I mean—' His brain wasn't working properly. 'I've deliberately been alone for a long time. I haven't wanted to be anything different. Yet here I am—by accident. An us.'

Ana's gaze sharpened. 'But not a romantic "us". Not a relationship "us".'

Was she asking for clarification because that was what she wanted? Or because she didn't?

'I don't know, Ana,' he said. 'Meeting you… and now having a baby with you… My life is upside down. Everything has changed.'

Ana was breathing faster—he watched the rise and fall of her chest. God knew his own heart was beating a million miles an hour.

'Is that what you want?' he asked her. 'A relationship with me?'

Ana was fiddling with the hem of her shirt, wrapping her fingers in the fabric, lifting it just high enough that he could see a sliver of her belly.

Was he wrong to be turned on by her naked skin when he'd told her he had nothing to offer beyond *wanting* her? Needing her?

'I don't know either,' Ana said. 'I don't really trust my judgement when it comes to relationships at the moment. I know I don't want to make another mistake…'

Those words were enough to snap him out of his fog. 'I can't promise you I won't be another mistake,' he said honestly. 'I'm not a good bet, Ana.'

With that, Ana stepped away. She turned her back, her gaze fixated on her cookie dough. Then she swore—something in Slavic, under her breath.

The next moment she was in his arms.

Oh, she'd missed this.

It was only weeks since Ana had last kissed Rhys, but to feel his mouth against hers again was *everything*. Hot and sexy and *perfect*.

Even though she knew kissing him was all types of *imperfect*.

Rhys kissed her back, in all the delicious ways he always did, but then his hands landed on her waist and moved no further.

He pushed her from him. Her hands fell away from where they'd been entwined behind his neck. He didn't push her far—she could still feel his breath on her lips. But it was far enough.

'Ana?'

She gazed into Rhys's eyes.

'If the last few days—or even years—have taught me anything, it's that life can change dramatically in an instant. So I should do the sensible thing here, and not kiss you again. Because we need to be mature grown-ups and raise a child together, and if we end up hating each other, that could be awkward.'

Rhys's lips kicked up in a crooked smile. He was utterly gorgeous. He hadn't shaved today, and his hair was definitely not neatly slicked back like it had been last night.

She liked this Rhys better—especially this close to her, with his height and broad shoulders making her kitchen feel small, making *Ana* feel small. He was all strength and power...and so much more.

'I don't know a lot right now...' Ana said. Had her voice ever sounded so husky? 'I don't know how we're going to work out this parenting thing, or if Mirjana will pull off her PR coup, or if I'll be universally hated by the people of Vela Ada. And I *definitely* don't know if this'll be a huge mistake.' She paused. 'But I *do* know that you want me. I do know that I want *you*. It's pretty definitive, isn't it?'

Rhys's hands gripped her waist harder, as if he was stopping himself from moving them, pulling her closer. And her own hands shook, she realised, from the effort not to touch him.

'I feel like I want to go with what I know right now,' Ana continued, 'rather than what *might* happen, or what I *might* know in the future. And

I think I want to feel the way you make me feel right now. Because the way you make me feel feels so *right*.'

'*Everything* about you feels right, Ana,' Rhys said.

His hands started to move, tracing the curve of her waist, her hips, and then curving over her backside as he tugged her close against him.

Now it was Ana's turn to grin. She trailed her fingers from the notch at the base of his neck along his collarbone, over the bulk of his shoulder, his biceps…then slid them over to the hard plane of his belly, curving under the fabric of his T-shirt.

She'd dropped her head to follow the journey of her fingertips and felt Rhys's breath hot against the sensitive skin behind her ear.

'Wanting you feels right, Ana,' he said, his words a rumble against her skin. 'After so many years of everything feeling wrong.'

His lips were against her neck, hot on her skin, and he was kissing his way to her jaw, tilting her chin upwards with one hand as his other dragged her body flush against his.

Then his mouth claimed hers again, and she claimed his right back.

CHAPTER FOURTEEN

ONCE AGAIN RHYS found himself waking in Ana's bed—before Ana.

Her bedroom was on the top floor of her villa and it was large and airy, with a four-poster bed draped in sheer white fabric. It was dark outside, although Rhys didn't think it was all that late. But he'd have to find his phone to check the time, and he had no interest in getting out of bed.

Now that it was dark the room was lit by—of all things—a Christmas tree. It wasn't particularly big, and it sat on a small round table in the corner of the room, its simple white globes providing just enough light for Rhys to watch Ana as she slept.

Last time they'd done this he'd deliberately ended it by calling Ana *Your Highness*. But, looking at her now, her title was the last thing on his mind. It wasn't a princess who lay beside him, naked except for the sheet around her middle, her bare arms and legs lovely and golden, but *Ana*.

The woman he was having a baby with.

The woman who'd changed everything.

Who made him feel *right*.

So, no, he wasn't going to be exiting the bed the way he had back in Castelrotto. At least, not right now.

But what *would* happen next? It was all well and good for him and Ana to be open and honest and everything, but what did any of it *mean*? Was this a one-off?

As he stared at the woman beside him, that seemed an impossibility.

The woman he was having a baby with.

Not for the first time, the enormity of that was almost overwhelming. His entire life had changed in an instant. Again.

Rhys lay on his side, with the same sheet that was rucked up around Ana's waist equally haphazardly spread across him. She was facing him as she slept, her breathing slow and regular.

It hadn't been a lie when he'd said it to Ana, but it was only now that his words really settled deep inside him, became irrevocably true:

Wanting Ana felt so right.

And also *this* felt right. Lying here beside her.

Beyond the attraction, the lust, their need for each other, *this* felt right.

Lying here with her. Being with her.

So what did that mean?

Ana shifted in her sleep.

She was so perfect. And he was such a mess. Five years of mess—a ruined career, isolation and, at his lowest points, bouts of intense anxiety.

Once, he would have told himself he could never hurt the people he loved. But he'd been doing exactly that for years. If he got out of bed to check the time, he would see yesterday's missed call notification still waiting for him. He never cleared the notifications immediately, letting them sit there like little guilty thumbtacks pressed into his brain.

Missed call. Mum.

But eventually he'd swipe across the screen and the notifications would be gone. At least now he didn't have the reminder of unread voicemail messages—he'd simply removed voicemail from his phone service.

That was when his mum and dad had started writing old-fashioned letters. Not emails, but *letters*—maybe because they'd guessed he wouldn't be able to throw them away?

His family did know him well, after all.

Well, they knew the old version of Rhys. The one from before. Ana had been right to challenge his commitment to their child. Because he *wasn't* the old Rhys any more—the one who'd rung his mum every week and never missed a family gathering.

He'd told Ana he wouldn't abandon their child and he'd meant it. He would move heaven and earth to be the best father he could be.

He wanted to do *more* than just cope now. He wanted to live. He wanted to...*love.*

Love his child.

Love—

No. For now he'd just focus on what he knew he could do. He knew he could—already *did*—love this child.

Ana and this baby had catapulted him beyond just existing in his life. Beyond just coping. And yet when his mother had called earlier today, he'd let it ring out. Answering her call hadn't even been an option.

Which told Rhys that, despite Ana, despite their baby, he was still broken.

He'd been broken for so very long.

He was going to patch himself together

enough to be a good father—he *was*—but was he capable of more than that? Or was he just too damaged? Were the fissures too deep?

Was this version of Rhys all he'd ever have to offer anyone? To offer Ana?

After all Ana had been through, was it fair to burden her with that? With him?

Ana stirred in her sleep, rolling onto her belly, her hair cascading over her bare shoulders in waves of chocolate brown.

Her eyes fluttered open and met his gaze, which he knew must be full of complications.

But Ana just smiled, then shimmied up onto her knees so she could look down at him, her long hair tickling his chest.

'Stop thinking,' she said. 'This works best when we go with what we *feel*.'

The old Rhys would probably have said they needed to talk. But this version of him selfishly dragged her onto his chest and followed Ana's advice to the letter.

Because when he kissed Ana, he wasn't capable of thinking about anything messy or painful or broken.

When he kissed Ana, he wasn't capable of thinking of anything but how good, how perfect—how *right*—she felt.

* * *

It was the carollers that woke Ana.

She'd dozed off again, with Rhys sprawled beside her, but now the sounds of Christmas carols drifted up from the street below.

The song that had woken her was a traditional Slavic carol, and the familiar melody made Ana smile as she remembered so many wonderful Christmases with her family—her *dida* playing the accordion beside her *baba*'s open fireplace, the smell of fir and baked treats filling their home...

Baking.

Her cookies!

Ana leapt out of bed, searching about for her clothes.

What time was it?

She retrieved her knickers from the bedroom floor and hopped into them as she raced into the kitchen. Thankfully she hadn't had a batch of cookies baking when she'd kissed Rhys. *Vrag* knew she'd forgotten all about them the instant he'd kissed her back. But she needed to finish all those cookies *tonight*—ready to take to the library tomorrow morning, for Christmas Eve.

T-shirt located, and then her phone, she tugged

the shirt over her head and checked the time: it was late, but she still had plenty of time.

Hands on her hips, she took a long, deep breath.

What was she doing?

And she wasn't just thinking about her baking.

Rhys was naked and sleeping in her bedroom. Her lips still felt deliciously bruised from his mouth, and her skin scratched from his stubble. If she closed her eyes and thought about what they'd just done, she'd be caught up in memories and sensations that were too good to regret.

And yet it had been a pretty dumb thing to do.

She'd said all the right things last night, but all sleeping with Rhys had done was make her wonder about *more*. Because surely sex couldn't be that intense, that intimate, but not mean anything?

She didn't think she was wired for casual sex—she never had been. But the couple of relationships she'd had before Petar had been short-lived—and certainly hadn't left her feeling like this. They hadn't been *anything* like this thing with Rhys, where attraction seemed to overwhelm her common sense.

Although she didn't exactly have a stellar

track record when it came to good judgement. She'd almost married the wrong man, after all…

Ana's eyes popped open. She didn't have any time to worry about Rhys right now. She had a *lot* of cookies to bake.

Rhys walked out of her bedroom just as she was putting the last tray of *medenjaci* into the oven. He wore his jeans, but nothing else—and he looked so remarkable without his shirt that Ana was momentarily helpless to do anything but stare at him.

'Hey,' he said. His gaze took in the kitchen and the rows of cookies on cooling racks. 'Looks like you've been busy.'

Ana closed the oven door and set the timer before turning to face Rhys properly. 'I have,' she said. 'They're for the kids at the library,' she explained. 'I decided I *would* make them again this year.'

After telling Rhys about *medenjaci* a few days ago, it had occurred to Ana there was no reason she *couldn't* bake them this year. So she'd organised a visit to her old workplace—with cookies—for tomorrow.

Rhys had located his shirt and jumper on the

floor near her sofa, but he didn't put either on. Instead he just stood there, looking at her.

Ana knew she must look a mess, with her hair all over the place and without a bra, and yet Rhys's gaze could only be described as admiring.

No, that was too gentle a word. When Rhys looked at her like that, it was as if he couldn't get enough of her. It was as if his gaze *devoured* her.

She suspected the way she looked at him wasn't all that different. All rumpled and sleepy and sexy, Rhys had never looked more handsome.

So, their sleeping together again had made no difference to the delicious magnetic pull between them.

Had she ever thought it would?

No. It had never even been a possibility.

'What happens now?' Ana asked bluntly.

Rhys looked down at his clothes. He'd bunched them into a tight ball.

'I told myself I was going to get dressed and go,' he said, even though he made no move to do so. He looked up and caught Ana's gaze. 'But what I really want is to kiss you again. I want to take you back to bed.'

His words, his gaze, made Ana catch her breath. The way Rhys wanted her was overwhelming. No other man had ever needed her the way Rhys did. It was a seductive and powerful sensation.

'I want that too,' she said, helpless not to. A blush heated her cheeks at her candour—but, honestly, what was the point of pretending otherwise? 'But—'

Suddenly Rhys was right in front of her, his hands at her hips, close enough that she had to look up at him—close enough to kiss.

He was doing it on purpose, of course, knowing his proximity to her scrambled her thoughts.

'How about—rather than thinking about how complicated this is, or about making mistakes, or about what we have ahead of us—we *both* take your advice and stop thinking when it comes to *us*,' he said, leaning closer until his lips were a whisper against her neck. 'When it comes to *this*.'

He kissed her, his mouth and his breath hot and electrifying against her skin. She shivered beneath his touch.

He murmured against that delicious spot just beneath her ear. 'You're the one who told me this works best when we go with what we *feel*.'

Ana made herself shake her head. 'We can't do that for ever.'

He took a step back now so he could meet her gaze. His expression was intense...serious. 'But what if we don't want for ever?' he said. 'What if we just worry about right now?'

His words held echoes of last night—focusing on what they both wanted in the moment and nothing more.

It was so tempting.

But it was so reckless.

Rhys leant forward again so his cheek was pressed against hers, his words rough against her ear.

'I know I don't want to walk away yet, Ana. I know I have to, and I know I *should*, but I can't. Not yet.'

Temptation warred with fear: Ana knew it would be all too easy to fall for Rhys. To be hurt by Rhys. And yet...

'I can't walk away either,' Ana said.

And barely had the words come out of her mouth than Rhys's mouth had covered hers and his hands had drawn her hard against him.

Sometime later—minutes? Hours? Ana had no idea—they came up for air.

Rhys just looked at her, waiting as they both took deep, shaky breaths.

'Stay the night,' she said.

The next moment Rhys swung Ana into his arms, exactly the way she'd imagined that very first night they'd met—as if saving her from a burning building. Then, as he carried her into her bedroom so effortlessly, Ana focused on all the heat, the *fire* between them—how irresistible it was, how powerful, how *right*...

All she needed to do was make sure she didn't get burned.

CHAPTER FIFTEEN

RHYS WOKE SUDDENLY to Ana shaking his
shoulder.

'Wake up!' she said in an urgent whisper. 'I
need your help.'

Instantly he was on his feet, his muscles coiled
and ready for action.

'What's wrong?' he asked sharply.

His gaze travelled over her—she was in jeans
and a pale blue button-up shirt and looked a bit
surprised, but not upset. The house was silent.
Outside, he heard a car drive by, but otherwise
all seemed calm.

'Nothing's wrong,' Ana said. 'It's just we both
slept in. I need help icing cookies.'

Adrenalin eased from his tense muscles. 'So
no emergency?' he said.

'No,' she said. 'Sorry... I didn't think that a
soldier might be used to emergencies more significant than those cookie-related.'

Rhys sank back onto the bed. He was completely naked and his hands were twisted in the white sheets.

'Are you okay?' Ana asked. Her forehead was creased with concern.

Not really.

For a split second he'd been back in the desert, hearing the worst possible news of his life. But Ana didn't want to hear that. She didn't *need* to hear that.

'Of course,' he said casually. 'You just startled me.'

For a moment he thought she wasn't going to leave it at that—that she was going to start asking questions.

But instead she smiled. It was her princess smile—he'd learnt to recognise it now. Practised, beautiful—and very fake.

He should be disgusted at himself for not walking away last night. Worse—for talking Ana into continuing a relationship based entirely on lust and attraction when he knew absolutely that Ana deserved so much more.

But he couldn't regret what he'd done. Couldn't regret being here with Ana.

And now, seeing her princess smile and her lack of questions, Rhys knew they were playing the same game.

She was going to pretend that she *hadn't* just triggered the worst memory of his life, and he was going to ignore that long-forgotten part of him that wanted to tell her everything.

In a relationship without a future, there wasn't much point digging up the past.

'Mirjana called earlier,' she said brightly. 'Just to confirm my visit to the City Library. She suggested you accompany me, as it's not an official royal visit, so there aren't the usual protocols. It will make our relationship appear quite serious.'

'Surely she knows I stayed here last night?' he asked.

'She might,' Ana said, 'but she didn't say a word. It's a perk of being royalty—the palace staff are unfailingly discreet.'

'So she's stage-managing a fake relationship around our *actual* relationship?'

'Well...' Ana said, and her tone was light. 'She's stage-managing a *serious* relationship, while I'd like this one to remain a secret as much as possible.'

Rhys had to laugh. 'This all feels a bit meta.'

Ana frowned. 'Meta?'

'Like a movie inside a movie,' he said. 'Or

arguing about arguing. We have a relationship inside a relationship.'

Or a non-relationship inside a fake relationship.

'Either way,' Ana said, 'I need you to help me ice these cookies.'

Ana's visit to the Vela Ada City Library hadn't been announced to the public, so there were a few glorious minutes after Ana walked through the familiar glass doors when no one noticed her arrival.

Her guards had already completed a covert sweep of the building, and now they kept their distance as Rhys and Ana stood just inside the library entrance, each balancing several boxes of *medenjaci* in their arms.

How had she described her love of libraries to Rhys?

There aren't many places where you can just be.

A familiar feeling of comfort and acceptance enveloped Ana as she walked towards the information desk. For those brief moments she could almost pretend she was still normal old Ana Tomasich, arriving for work. Ana Tomasich—

who no one looked twice at and who was perfectly happy with her perfectly average life.

But by the time her once colleague and meant-to-be bridesmaid Anita had greeted her, half the library *had* looked twice. And the other half had by the time Rhys shook Anita's hand.

The change in the library was palpable.

No longer was everyone happily browsing the shelves, or searching the web, or reading the newspaper. Everyone was looking at *her*. Talking about *her*.

It was impossible to hear exactly what people were actually saying, but Ana could imagine…

Did you know she used to work here? I wonder why she—

Her poor fiancé. I heard—

What a lovely dress. I bet it cost more than I earn in a month—

The buzz and hum of conversation, of speculation, was impossible to ignore, and Ana heard clearer snippets as Anita led the way to the children's corner.

Fancy flaunting a new man so soon—

Probably thinks she's better than us now—

Suddenly Rhys took her hand in his. Calmly he laced his fingers with hers and then gently squeezed her palm.

Immediately the buzz of real and imagined judgement receded. Partly because Rhys's touch was as electric and distracting as always, but mostly because of the way he looked at her.

He looked at her as if he could see all that ricocheted inside her brain at that very moment, and none of it mattered to him. Because of course it didn't—Rhys North couldn't care less what strangers thought of him, or of her.

In that moment, as Rhys looked at her, Ana felt as if all that Rhys cared about was the fact she knew he was here, beside her. Both literally and...*more*.

We're in this together.

For the first time she actually believed it. They weren't simply words said to reassure, they were real. A fact.

What did Rhys keep saying? That they were an *us* now.

Right now she didn't care about defining what that meant. All that mattered was that it was true, and that Rhys was beside her.

And then they were with the kids, and the small group of children cross-legged on the floor stared at Ana as if... Well, as if she was a princess.

Anita introduced Ana to the children, and

then Ana was in charge—getting Rhys to help open the boxes of *medenjaci* and then distributing the undecorated cookies to the children.

She'd organised for a table to be set up with decorating supplies—royal icing, edible glitter and chocolate pearls, all in a myriad of colours—and before she knew it she was helping the girls and boys decorate their cookies, and they were telling her all about what they hoped to get for Christmas.

She couldn't help but get caught up in their excitement, even though she realised now that she'd naively expected today to be just like it had always been—as if she was still a librarian and could decorate Christmas cookies with pink icing without the library's patrons snapping photos of her with their smartphones.

But that didn't matter—not really.

She was having fun, and the kids were too.

Later, with the creatively decorated biscuits carefully wrapped up for each child to take home, the librarians distributed the remainder of the cookies she'd made to everyone else in the library. These were the *medenjaci* she'd decorated with Rhys, although he'd been relegated to the positioning of chocolate pearls.

This left Rhys and Ana alone beneath the chains of paper angels that hung from the ceiling, and beside a table full of shoeboxes containing Plasticine nativity scenes.

'What are these?' Rhys asked, walking to the plates that covered a wide windowsill.

'Pšenica,' Ana said. 'We did it for the first time last year. It's just wheat in saucers, but the tradition is that the taller your wheat by Christmas, the luckier you'll be the following year.'

Rhys grinned. 'Can you use fertiliser?'

Ana laughed. 'Now, why didn't I think of that last Christmas?'

'Oprostite?'

The soft *excuse me* came from a young girl aged eight or nine, standing beside her mother only a few metres away. In her hands, the girl clutched her decorated biscuits.

Ana smiled and beckoned her over.

'Can my mother take a photo of me with you?' the girl asked shyly.

'Of course!' Ana said, and Rhys stepped aside as Ana knelt beside the girl and smiled for her mother's phone camera.

'Thank you,' the girl's mother said a few minutes later. 'Ajla still has that newspaper article from last year on her wall. You've made her Christmas with this new photo.'

It took Ana a moment to work out what the woman was talking about—but then she remembered. In early December last year—before she had become a princess—Ana had been photographed with some children at the library for an article about their upcoming Christmas craft workshops. Ajla must have been one of those children.

'But you weren't *really* a princess back then,' Ajla said, any trace of her original reticence gone, 'so my friend Lara said it didn't count. But now I have a photo with a *real* princess. I can't *wait* to show her.'

The other woman's cheeks turned a heated pink. 'Ajla!' she said sharply. 'I'm *so* sorry, Your Highness—'

Ana waved her apology away. 'Don't be silly,' she said. She crouched down again, to be at Ajla's eye level. 'I'm still the same person,' she said to the little girl. 'Becoming a princess hasn't changed who I am.'

But Ajla was clearly unconvinced, and by now there was a short queue of children, waiting—hoping—for photos too.

As Ana posed with the girls and boys, it was

impossible not to compare the nondescript woman who'd been in that newspaper article and the woman who now had children staring at her adoringly.

Was she still the same person she'd been a year ago?

When she'd walked into the library today, she'd wanted desperately to be Ana Tomasich again. But now, as she smiled a *real* smile—not her princess smile—she wondered... Did she *really* want to give all this up?

Not the adulation she was receiving from these beautiful children—she still felt a bit uncomfortable being seen as special just because of an accident of birth—but the rest of what came with her title.

For example, just beyond the children's corner here in the library there was a new display stand for talking books. A similar stand was in every library on the island—thanks to her. It was a small thing. Just a start. But to have the means to make a difference in that way was a gift. A privilege.

And beyond that display stand—in the nonfiction section, shelved almost exactly as they had been twenty years ago—was a row of books about the Vela Ada royal family. Ana couldn't see those books from here, of course, but she knew they were there. And she also knew that some day soon—if not already—new books in that section would include *her* name on their pages. *Her* name. Ana Tomasich—Princess Ana of Vela Ada.

She'd finally found the belonging she'd searched for in those history books all those years ago in the foyer of Palace Vela Ada, only days ago. Found the part of her she hadn't even fully realised she'd been missing—the other half of her heritage. No matter what her father had done, she was a part of the royal family now. It was part of who she was.

So, no. She *wouldn't* change any of this. She *didn't* want to go back to her old life. And she'd been wrong when she'd told Ajla she was the same person she'd always been.

Oh, she was still Ana Tomasich—she always would be. But this past year *had* changed her. For all her missteps and mistakes, she'd grown into her new identity—into her new reality.

She had wondered, as she'd run away from her wedding only weeks ago, if her title would ever sit comfortably on her shoulders. But now, as she laughed and posed in the library—always aware of Rhys watching her with his electric gaze—she realised it was no longer about her title: if she should have accepted it, if it would ever fit.

Now it was just who she was: Princess Ana of Vela Ada.

After all the children had left and once again it was Rhys and Ana alone—the library now almost empty—Ana looked up at Rhys and smiled.

And for the first time in a year, she had absolutely no doubts. She knew who she was, she knew where she belonged—and she knew what she wanted.

Rhys North. For however long it lasted.

Something had happened at the library. When they'd arrived, Ana had been nervous and unsure beside him—but when they'd left, she'd been the Ana he'd become familiar with. The Ana who was all spark and quiet determination.

He'd been watching her all day, unable to let his gaze drift far from her. In her tailored dress and perfectly coiffed hair she'd looked one hundred per cent royal—and the way she'd interacted with the patrons of the library had been one hundred per cent pure princess. Had she finally realised? That she *was* a princess, and worthy of the title she'd told him she didn't think she deserved?

He itched to talk to her about it now, as they drove through narrow, winding lanes to a small town a short distance outside of the capital city.

It was dark outside—it was late, of course, given they were driving to Midnight Mass. Ana sat silently beside him, although they *had* been talking before. They'd been talking all afternoon, actually. After they'd left the library and met with Mirjana at the palace for another briefing, and while having dinner with Prince Marko and Princess Jasmine. They'd had a great day, really, talking easily and enjoying each other's company.

But it had been determinedly light. No discussion about his obvious fright that morning, and likewise no questions about what Rhys thought had changed at the library.

But then, maybe he'd imagined it anyway.

Ana reached out then, her fingertips brushing against the outside of his thigh, and his skin was suddenly hot beneath the wool of his suit. He halted her hand, gripping it in his and meeting her gaze before briefly darting his eyes to the driver and the bodyguard in the front seat.

They were both looking straight ahead, but he was sure if he did what he *wanted* to do—which was to drag Ana onto his lap—he'd very quickly have their attention.

'Ana—' he said, but it was more a rough plea than an admonishment.

He wanted nothing more than to have her hands on his body, and his on hers—but this was not the place, and he was barely able to control himself around her as it was.

It had been like this since they'd left the library. Subtle and not so subtle touches, with Ana leading the way. Her hand on his arm, his hips, his legs, and once—memorably—on his butt...

Only when no one could see, but it was driving him insane.

'We're about to go to *church*, Ana,' he said.

She grinned. 'But *then* we'll go home.'

Somehow he kept himself together as they arrived at the small church, located close to Ana's grandparents' place. Ana's attendance there had been kept secret, and they entered the church at the last possible moment, nodding a greeting to Vesna and her parents as they took their places beside them in the back pew.

After mass, Christmas carollers greeted the

crowd that spilled outside, each singer holding a candle that flickered in the moonlight.

Ana spoke in Slavic as she introduced him to her grandparents, so he had no idea what she said. But they smiled at him and wished him a merry Christmas in the little English they knew.

It was officially Christmas now, Rhys realised, and it felt like the most natural thing in the world to put his arm around Ana and draw her close against his side.

She looked up at him, and when she did everything else faded away—the sound of the carollers, the many people taking photos of them, even Ana's family.

'Merry Christmas, Rhys,' she said.

'Merry Christmas, Ana,' he replied.

And as he spoke, he realised they weren't just meaningless words, said only because they were expected. Christmas *wasn't* going to be just another day this year.

A sensation he'd thought he'd never experience again at Christmas had sneaked up on him—unexpected, but not unwelcome. But it was unquestionably what he was feeling as he looked at Ana amongst the carols and the candlelight.

Joy.

CHAPTER SIXTEEN

HOW HAD SHE possibly lasted so long without kissing Rhys?

It felt like days, not hours.

The moment Ana's front door had closed behind them she was in his arms, and he was kissing her before they'd even taken off their coats and scarves.

His mouth was hot and intent and *incredible* against hers, and his hands as they shoved off her outer layers of clothing were strong and electric against her skin.

Somehow they were upstairs, and then in her bedroom, on her bed, finally with no clothes at all, and his weight was heavy and delicious and *exactly* what she needed above her...inside her.

Later, she woke to go to the bathroom, and then, wrapped in a silk dressing gown, she ventured out into the living room to turn off forgotten lights. She collected their clothes as she went, eventually making her way downstairs and retrieving their discarded coats.

She hung them in the small closet in the foyer, and as she did so the familiar sound of a vibrating phone emanated from the pocket of Rhys's navy blue coat.

She fished it out…turned it over in her hand to see who was calling.

It had rung out before she could even wonder if she should answer, and the screen changed from a ringing phone to a notification.

Five missed calls. Mum.

Instantly Ana was rushing up the stairs and back to her room—although she paused for a moment as she sat on the edge of the bed, remembering Rhys's reaction that morning.

She didn't really want to shake him awake and cause that awful look of grief and horror in his eyes again. But what if his mother was calling about an emergency? Five missed calls *meant* something. Someone only called that often if they *had* to get in touch.

So she laid her hand on his shoulder and pushed gently. 'Rhys,' she said, soft but firm. 'Wake up, *dragi moj.*'

The Slavic endearment—*my dear one*—had

just slipped out, but Ana didn't have time to worry about that as Rhys jerked awake.

'What's wrong?' he said urgently. He was already sitting up, his muscles tense. 'Are you okay?'

'I'm fine,' she said. 'But I found your phone when I was tidying up our clothes. Your mother is trying to call you. She's called five times,' she said carefully. 'It must be something important.'

Or something wrong.

She so hoped it wasn't. Rhys had already been through so much…

But rather than look concerned, Rhys let his whole body relax. In fact, he fell back against the pillows, his face a picture of relief.

'No,' Rhys said, 'nothing's wrong.' He grinned at her, reaching for her hand. 'Come back to bed.'

Ana shook her hand free. 'How do you know nothing's wrong?' she said. 'She's called *five times.*'

'She's only called a few times *today,*' he said. 'The other calls are from yesterday.'

But now his whole demeanour had changed. He rubbed at his forehead as Ana sat stiffly on the edge of the mattress. Suddenly all she could think about was that box full of unopened envelopes in his pantry in Castelrotto.

'Were you planning on calling her back?' Ana said.

Rhys met her gaze, and his eyes didn't waver. 'No,' he said.

'Why not?' Ana said. 'What if something's wrong?'

'Nothing's wrong,' Rhys repeated. And before she could ask again how he knew that, he added, 'Because if there was, she would've called my assistant. I had her provide her details to my family years ago.'

'You had *her* provide her details?'

Rhys shrugged, but it was far from a casual movement. 'Living like that has been the only way I've been able to cope, Ana,' he said. 'I told you—'

Ana shook her head as she stood up, backing away from him.

'I saw the letters, Rhys,' she said. 'In your kitchen. I didn't mean to—I knocked them off a shelf accidentally, and I didn't know what they meant until later.' She swallowed. 'I didn't realise they meant you'd abandoned your family until the night we had dinner. And then I was stupid enough to believe you when you told me you hadn't abandoned them at all.'

Rhys leapt to his feet, crossing the short distance between them until he stood close enough for Ana to touch him. Although of course she didn't.

'It was my way of *surviving*,' he said, his voice low and harsh.

Something Rhys had said echoed in Ana's memory: *'If my anxiety becomes a problem, I'll deal with it properly this time. Not go hide on a mountain.'*

'How hard have you tried over the past five years to find a way to cope—to grieve—that *didn't* mean hurting the people you love?'

He was angry now. 'You don't *get* it,' he said. 'Don't you think I would've found another way if I could? Do you think it's been *easy* to isolate myself from the family I had left? If there was *any* other option that didn't paralyse me with panic, don't you think I would have taken it? That I'd have grabbed it with both hands and run all the way back to Melbourne with it?'

Ana crossed her arms in front of her body. Rhys was naked, and she watched as he took deep breaths, his chest rising and falling in rapid movements.

'So you've been seeing a doctor who can help you?' she asked. But she already knew the answer.

He ran a hand through his hair, leaving it spiked all over the place. 'No,' he said flatly.

'The other night,' Ana began, 'when you told me why you've been living the way you have, I didn't really get what it meant. I mean, I understood what it meant for *you*—and, Rhys, I get that you did what you needed to do to get through each day. I get it... I understand it. But last night I didn't put myself in your mother's shoes. I didn't imagine how it would feel to call your son, to write to your son, *to want your son in your life*—and get nothing back.'

Ana couldn't look at him now, so she hugged herself, staring at the little Christmas tree she'd set up in the corner of her room. Its lights were blurry through the tears she fought to contain.

'The thing is, Rhys, now that I've put myself in her shoes—well, it feels pretty familiar. And you know what it feels like? Rejection. And *Vrag* knows I'm familiar enough with *that*.'

Rhys reached out for her, but she stopped the movement with a glare.

'I meant what I told you last night,' Rhys

said. 'I've changed. I want more than just to cope now. Since I met you, Ana, everything's changed.'

Ana nodded. 'How?' she prompted. '*How* have things changed? What steps are you taking so that your relationships aren't destroyed by your anxiety, Rhys? Your relationships with your family, with your child, with…' She almost didn't say it, but in the end she had to. 'Your relationship with *me*.'

His gaze locked on hers. 'My relationship with you?'

The time was long past for Ana to protect herself from being hurt, from being burned. She nodded. And as she did, she saw something in his gaze. Hope? Fear? Despair?

She had no idea, because he locked it all away before she could interpret it.

His voice was steadier when he spoke again. Without the rawness of before. 'I haven't had an attack in years, Ana. I *do* have it under control.'

But he didn't. Ana knew that now.

Still, she felt compelled to confirm it—to underline it in ink: 'Have you told your family I'm pregnant?' she asked.

His eyes widened. 'Of course not,' he said.

Of course not.

Ana nodded. 'You haven't told them anything about me—that's why your mother is calling you a lot recently. She's probably seen the news reports and wants to know what on earth is going on. But you won't answer her calls.'

Rhys didn't have to nod—didn't have to say a thing.

Ana closed her eyes and took a long, deep breath. She'd been so stupid. So very, very stupid. To get caught up in lust and attraction and in believing meaningless words about how she'd *changed* him.

'I think you should leave, Rhys,' she said quietly.

'Ana,' he said fiercely, 'I *will* be there for our child. I *will* be a good father. I promise you that.'

Oh, she so wanted to believe him.

'For our child's sake, I'm going to take you at your word—for now.'

And if Rhys *ever* hurt their child…if he abandoned their child the way he'd abandoned his family…the way her father had abandoned *her*…

She'd never forgive him.

And she'd never forgive herself.

She had no choice but to give him a chance

to do the right thing. She had to give her child a chance at having a father.

But she *did* have a choice when it came to her own relationship with Rhys.

She was supposed to be *living in the moment* with him—it was what they'd agreed, after all—but she'd been lying to herself. Right from the start—from the *moment* he'd touched her—she'd just kept on wanting more. More of Rhys. More *from* Rhys.

He'd told her from the outset that he wasn't capable of being her Prince. She'd told him she didn't want one, and she still didn't.

She didn't want a prince.

She wanted Rhys.

But not like this.

More than anything, Ana wanted to be loved.

But Rhys's love consisted of unopened envelopes, ignored invitations and phone calls that went unanswered.

That wasn't the type of love she wanted in her life.

But—significantly—Rhys wasn't even offering her that. He wasn't reassuring her that he'd be there for *her*, that he'd be a good partner. His relationship with her wasn't even on his radar.

Because they didn't have one.

'I think you should leave, Rhys,' Ana repeated softly.

As she watched, Rhys dressed quietly.

Then, without another word to her, he was gone.

CHAPTER SEVENTEEN

NOT VERY MANY hours and hardly any sleep later, Rhys sat at Prince Marko and Princess Jasmine's dining table, in a room that would rival a department store window for its sheer volume of tinsel and baubles. Christmas carols played in the background as palace staff served a sumptuous Christmas morning feast, and Rhys drank a *lot* of coffee in a futile attempt to shift his fog of exhaustion.

Although Rhys knew it wasn't really a lack of sleep that weighed him down. Far heavier were the memories of last night—memories of Ana's shock and disappointment.

Her hurt.

And also what that hurt *meant*. He knew Ana's priority was their child, but it was more than that—she'd even said it: *their relationship*.

For a moment—a fleeting moment—the same joy he'd felt outside the church as he'd looked at Ana amongst the carollers had bloomed, even bigger than before. Because in that moment he'd imagined what it might be like to be loved by Ana. Maybe for that fleeting second he'd even seen it in her gaze.

But then he'd remembered.

Remembered that he was broken. That he couldn't even answer a call from his mother, and that he fully intended to have his assistant inform his family that he was having a child with a princess.

And Ana deserved so much more than that.

She knew it too.

A present being passed across the table from Jasmine was a timely distraction.

'Is this for me?' Rhys asked, with some embarrassment. It hadn't even occurred to him to get Marko or Jas a gift. 'I have to apologise... I don't have anything for you.'

'Don't be silly,' Jas said. 'Besides, it's not really for you, anyway.'

And, as Rhys discovered when he opened the gift, it wasn't. It was a tiny baby's outfit, printed with whimsical suns and fluffy rain clouds.

'I have become rather obsessed with cute baby clothing,' Jas said. 'I don't know what's happened to me.' She grinned and rubbed her large round belly. 'I already have more than enough, besides my own shopping and the gifts the people of Vela Ada keep so generously giving us. So I grabbed the opportunity to go shopping for *your* baby.'

Rhys smiled and thanked Jas, placing the package amongst the Christmas crackers and candy canes scattered across the table. Then he managed to talk with Jasmine and Marko for the rest of breakfast like a normal person—about all things unimportant and silly jokes.

But the whole time he was counting down to when he'd see Ana again—only hours from now, for Christmas dinner.

The prospect of seeing her was tinged with both dread and anticipation. Anticipation because it was *Ana*, the woman who had changed everything even if she didn't believe it herself. Just thinking about her heated his blood, scrambled his thoughts. But he also felt dread, because now Ana knew how truly broken he was.

She was going to look at him differently tonight. Not with heat, and spark, and undeniable connection.

Tonight her eyes would be full of disappointment.

Disappointment in *him*.

For not being the man she'd thought he was.
For not being the man he'd once been.

Queen Petra bumped her shoulder against Ana's as they stood in front of the giant Christmas tree in the palace foyer. The royal photographer was checking the images he'd already taken on his camera, so the royal family were having a short break from posing for their annual official Christmas portrait.

'Are you *sure* there's not something going on between you and Mr North?' she asked.

King Lukas and Queen Petra had come home with Prince Filip and the Queen Dowager for the traditional royal family Christmas dinner. Lukas and Petra were fully aware of the situation, of course, but they'd met Rhys only about an hour ago. He stood to the side of one of the sweeping staircases, attempting to win over Ana's mother, and Ana's gaze kept darting in that direction.

Ana managed a careless smile. 'Yes,' she said. 'I *like* Rhys, but there's nothing else between us.'

Petra pursed her lips. 'Anyone with eyes doesn't believe that, Ana.'

Ana blinked, stunned. Petra had always been

refreshingly candid, but she hadn't expected *that* comment.

If anything, she'd been careful *not* to look at Rhys. She certainly hadn't touched him, nor really even spoken to him all night. Likewise, Rhys had kept his distance from her.

He'd been polite, and so had she, but nothing more.

Ana imagined that was the way things would work between them from now on. For the next eighteen or so years.

The prospect of such careful interaction for evermore was pretty awful, but what other choice did she have? That was assuming Rhys even stayed in her and their child's life, anyway. After last night she really had no reason to assume that he would.

Yet even now a part of her wanted to argue with herself: *Rhys is a good man. He would never abandon his child.*

And to think she thought she'd learnt from the rose-coloured Petar fairy tale. Clearly not. But at least this time she'd disentangled herself early. Before it became too serious. Too complicated.

But had she really?

Three nights with Rhys felt a lot more meaningful than a year with her former fiancé. Than *any* time she'd spent with any other man.

She gave herself a mental shake. What was she even *thinking*?

On her other side Princess Jasmine cleared her throat, and Ana turned to meet her gaze.

'My Slavic's still a bit rusty,' she said, 'but I think I got the gist of it and I agree with Petra.' Jas paused, then grinned. 'Also, FYI, I *really* like him. Plus, he's gorgeous, Ana. Nice choice.'

Ana understood that the two women meant well, and were just teasing, but their words made her tense and made tears prickle.

Stupid hormones.

But it was more than that—and she knew it.

'Ana?'

Petra was leaning closer now.

'I'm so sorry. I didn't mean to upset you. It's just the way he looks at you... I thought maybe...'

'Our situation is complicated,' Ana said firmly. 'But I can assure you nothing is going on between us.'

At least not any more.

Ana took a deep breath, straightened her shoulders, then focused her gaze once again on the photographer, ready to smile on cue.

* * *

Dinner was lovely. Well, the food was lovely. But with Rhys seated beside her—which made sense, as although the royal family was aware of the PR exercise the majority of palace staff were not—Ana felt as tightly coiled as a spring.

The effort to avoid bumping knees or elbows or fingers, or even to *look* at Rhys, was excruciating. On top of that, she could barely remember what kind of relationship she was pretending to portray. A happy couple for the palace staff? Just friends for Petra and Jasmine?

She definitely didn't want to portray the very real tension between them. And she certainly didn't want anyone to ask her what was wrong, as she was so worried the tears that had threatened during the family portrait would spring free all over her roast turkey.

But, equally, she couldn't pretend to be okay. She couldn't talk to Rhys as if last night had never happened—even the idea felt impossible.

Rhys appeared to be faring much better. Yes, she sensed he was avoiding touching or looking just as much as she was, but he was managing to participate in the conversation with his usual easy manner. In fact, he even made them all laugh as he and Marko regaled them with stories of their time training and working together.

Maybe it was only Ana who heard the emptiness in his laugh?

Or maybe she'd imagined it, the same way she'd imagined a connection between them that went beyond the physical.

That had felt real and right.

But of course she'd been totally wrong.

Somehow no one appeared to notice Ana's discomfort. Everyone was relaxed and merry—even Ana's mother, who had been seated a good distance from Rhys and had eventually stopped shooting him accusatory glares.

After Prince Filip had gone to bed they all moved to the Knights' Hall for *pršurate*—spicy, citrusy doughnut balls—and eggnog.

Conversation was boisterous, and Ana spent much of the evening talking to her mother and the Queen Dowager, and later with Petra and Jas—although this time no one asked her about Rhys.

Rhys, of course, kept his distance.

About halfway through Jasmine's telling of a story about her own first Christmas at Palace Vela Ada, Jas grimaced.

'Are you okay?' Ana asked.

Jas grinned, but it was unconvincing. 'I probably just ate too much,' she said. 'I might go and sit down for a bit...'

There was only room for two on the small antique sofa that Jas went to sit down on, so Ana left Petra to watch her sister-in-law and went to find her mother.

The Queen Dowager had immediately taken a liking to Vesna when the truth of Ana's parentage had been revealed, and had always made an effort to include Vesna in royal events. But Ana's mother wasn't with the Queen Dowager, who was currently talking to Rhys and her sons.

In fact, she wasn't in the Knights' Hall at all.

But Ana didn't have any time to think about that before a shriek distracted her.

'Oh, my God—I just wet myself!' Princess Jasmine said in disbelief.

'No,' Petra said quietly, 'I think your waters have broken.'

Marko was instantly at Jasmine's side. 'You're not due for five more weeks.'

Jasmine's eyes were wide, her expression a mixture of confusion and concern. 'I think we need to go to the hospital,' she said.

* * *

Minutes later, Ana and Rhys watched as two cars whisked Jasmine, Marko, Lukas, Petra and the Queen Dowager away.

They stood in their coats at the top of the palace steps. They were not really helping by being out there, but Ana hadn't been able to just sit around inside.

Soon the palace gates had closed behind the rear lights of the cars and it was just Rhys and Ana—alone for the first time that evening.

'You okay?' Rhys asked.

Ana realised that she was holding a hand over her still flat belly. 'Oh!' she said. 'Yes. I think...'

'You *think*?' His gaze darted over her, as if searching for something amiss.

Ana smiled. 'I'm fine,' she said. 'Just worried for Jasmine.' She wrapped her arms around herself. 'It's freezing. Let's go and wait for news inside.'

A palace attendant opened the doors for them and took their coats, but once inside Ana turned to speak to him.

'Have you seen my mother?' she asked.

Despite the hubbub of the past few minutes, Ana's mother had not appeared.

The grey-haired man's eyebrows drew together, and he paused before answering her. 'I believe she's gone to see the chef about the *pršurate* recipe, Your Highness,' he said.

Ana nodded. She should have guessed. These past few visits her mother had taken to scribbling down every palace recipe she'd enjoyed.

With the Knights' Hall being cleaned, Rhys and Ana were guided to a smaller salon. Thanks to the magic of the palace staff the room already had a crackling fire, and yet more pastries were laid out on a low table.

Ana immediately sat down on a red velvet chair beside the table and helped herself to a *pršurate*. But Rhys remained standing. He wore charcoal trousers, a crisp white shirt and no tie. He looked very handsome—but then, he always did.

The atmosphere in the small room was a tense mix of concern for Jasmine, echoes of the previous night and—frustratingly—the electric attraction that *still* hummed between them. Despite everything. And now they were finally alone that snap and crackle was only amplified.

Ana felt compelled to say something—to prove she was totally okay and ready to proceed with this new dynamic between them: two people who had had a brief relationship that was over, and who now needed to prepare to co-parent in a mature and respectful manner.

Unsurprisingly, the perfect thing to say did not immediately present itself.

Rhys shoved his hands into the front pockets of his trousers, took a few steps towards her, and then seemed to change his mind.

He cleared his throat. 'Ana,' he began, 'I—'

But whatever he had been about to say was derailed by a loud burst of male laughter outside the salon, immediately followed by the trill of feminine giggles.

Familiar feminine giggles.

'Majka?' Ana asked in disbelief as she leapt to her feet and took in the pair suddenly framed in the doorway.

Her mother stood with her arm hooked around the waist of a tall, dark-haired man that Ana immediately recognised—Ivan, Prince Marko's valet. And Ivan had his own arm wrapped around Vesna, her body pressed right up against his side.

Ivan immediately dropped his arm and took a small step away from Ana's mother.

'Your Highness—' he began.

But before he could say anything further

Vesna had grabbed Ivan's hand in hers, lacing her fingers with his.

Vesna looked up at Ivan, and in the look that passed between them, and especially in the way Ivan nodded and then smiled encouragingly, Ana could see exactly what was going on.

'Ivan and I are together,' Vesna said carefully. 'I'm sorry I didn't tell you earlier, but we wanted to be sure.'

Her mother's face was a mix of apprehension and... *joy.*

Ana couldn't quite believe it—but she also couldn't remember the last time she'd seen her mother so happy.

Maybe only the day Ana had become a princess. 'I'm so happy for you, Majka,' Ana said.

But then a buzzing noise distracted her, and Ana watched as Rhys fished his phone out of his pocket.

'It's Marko,' he said, looking at Ana just before he answered the call.

Ana quickly filled her mother and Ivan in on what had happened with Jasmine, and then they all turned to Rhys for news.

The call was brief.

'Jasmine is doing well,' Rhys said after he'd hung up. 'She hasn't gone into labour, but they're keeping her in hospital—under observation and on antibiotics to prevent infection.'

Ana let go of the breath she'd been holding.

'Oh, thank goodness,' Ana said, just as her mother and Ivan said exactly the same thing.

Then they all laughed, before Vesna took Ivan's hand in hers again.

'I won't need a lift home in the palace car,' she said to Ana.

And with that, as a blush stole up Vesna's neck, Ivan and Vesna exited the room.

For a while Ana just stared at the once again empty doorway. Then, slowly, she turned to face Rhys.

Relief and shock momentarily left her speechless.

Her mother and Ivan? She'd *never* have guessed. But then, this past year had been strange and different in so many ways, and one of the worst things was how little Ana had been sharing with her mother about how she'd been feeling. About becoming a princess, about Petar—even about her pregnancy.

But then, why *should* she have known about Ivan? Her mother was her own woman, and she owed Ana no explanation. Vesna deserved to be happy—more than anyone, really.

Suddenly, Ana laughed.

She laughed to release the tension of the day—the tension caused by her worry for Jasmine, the tension between her and Rhys, and even the tension caused by the guilt she was carrying for being a less than perfect princess for her mother—which she'd finally realised she needed to let go.

She also laughed to release the tension of this past week—of discovering her pregnancy, of telling Rhys, of telling the royal family, of comprehending the way she was going to be judged for falling pregnant so soon after jilting Petar.

And she laughed because just as Vesna deserved to be happy, so did Ana.

She was looking at the man who, amidst some of the most stressful times of her life, had made her laugh, made her feel strong, made her feel beautiful—and made her feel in ways she never had before. She couldn't regret meeting him, and she couldn't even regret these past few days, even as her heart hurt because she knew they'd never have anything more.

There was no romantic future between them. Ana knew that now.

But, despite everything, she knew he still

wanted her. She knew his attraction for her, and hers for him, was unchanged.

She could see the complications in his gaze. Had he seen what she was thinking in hers?

She could almost hear what he was going to say. Something designed to keep her at arm's length. He knew now that Ana wanted more from him, and she knew that he didn't want to hurt her.

But she didn't want Rhys to be considerate. She didn't want his pity.

'Don't think tonight, Rhys, please,' she said. 'I just want tonight. Nothing more.'

Right now, she needed Rhys. She needed to feel strong and beautiful and wanted—all the things she always felt with Rhys. She needed this man who had been a constant in the madness of the past month of her life, because she knew he could give her tonight.

She stepped towards him, giving him every opportunity to step back, to say something, to tell her no.

But he did none of those things.

Instead he met her halfway.

And when they kissed, as always, everything felt right.

CHAPTER EIGHTEEN

RHYS WOKE TO the sound of Ana getting dressed.

She stood at the end of his bed, lit only by the light she'd switched on in his en suite bathroom. As he watched, she stepped into her red dress, pulled it up over her stockings, and then slid the long sleeves over her arms. She twisted to do up the zip at the back, but despite her best efforts couldn't quite reach it, so the dress made soft swishing sounds as she twisted to and fro, her occasional low Slavic curses not appearing to help at all.

'Need a hand?' Rhys asked.

Ana startled. 'Oh,' she said, 'I thought you were sleeping.'

'Nope,' he said unnecessarily as he sat up in bed, the sheets gathered about his waist.

Ana studied him for a moment, then seemed to make a decision and walked over to present her back to him.

The zip began low, so the dress gaped open

and he had a view of lace underwear, her stockings and the lovely olive skin of her back, her spine a shadowy curve in the muted light.

Everything in him wanted to reach for her, to tug her gently so she was beside him on his bed, close enough that he could kiss his way along the same path the zip would travel.

But he didn't do that.

Instead he carefully gripped the tab of the zipper and slowly, carefully, slid it upwards. All the while pretending he didn't notice the way Ana was trembling beneath his touch.

'Thank you,' she said softly, when he was done.

She stepped away and walked towards the door.

This was it, then.

Ana was going to walk out of his room and it would be over.

What they'd had would be over.

From now on it would be just like today had been: polite and awkward and...terrible, really.

It had been near impossible to spend so much time with Ana today and not touch her. Not be able to lean close to talk to her. To brush his hand against her waist. To make her laugh or make her gaze turn hot.

But what other option did he have?

It said a lot about the type of man he'd become that he hadn't stopped Ana tonight. That he'd pushed aside his noble concerns about hurting this amazing woman as easily as he'd unzipped her dress.

He didn't deserve this woman.

He had nothing to offer her.

But he couldn't let her go. Not yet.

'Stay,' he said, as her hand gripped the door handle.

Ana went still.

'Why?' she said. She still faced the door.

Rhys pushed himself to his feet. 'I don't want you to go.'

She turned then, her lips quirking into something like a smile. 'But how long would I be staying for?'

'How about we just worry about tonight?'

Ana shook her head. 'No,' she said simply. 'We want different things.' She turned the handle, revealing a sliver of hallway light as the door cracked open. 'I want a proper relationship, Rhys. I don't want a relationship that we live in one-night increments, without a future.'

'But do we have to worry about that *now*, Ana?' Rhys said, stepping towards her. 'Why not just take it night by night? It's been working okay so far.'

The door cracked open further.

'So that's where you think we're heading, Rhys? To a proper relationship?'

There was no way he could lie to her. 'No,' he said.

Ana smiled another humourless smile. 'There you go,' she said, her voice suddenly very soft. 'As I said. We want different things.'

The door was open now. She was going to walk away.

'*No,*' Rhys said. 'We don't want different things.'

Ana froze, her gaze focused entirely on the door handle. 'You just said you didn't want a relationship with me.'

'No,' he clarified. 'Of *course* I want a relationship with you, Ana. It's like I told you. You're the only woman—the only *thing*—I've wanted in five years. I've just been *existing* for a very long time. With you, I feel alive. With you, I want everything. I want everything that we have together already: fun and laughter and sex and connection. And I want more. I want...'

He rubbed his forehead, squeezing his eyes

shut tight as he realised what he was about to say.

I want love.

He wanted to love Ana so badly. Maybe he already did. But the idea of saying those words again…

He just couldn't.

His eyes popped open. Ana hadn't moved, but now she was staring at him, her gaze locked on his.

'I can't have a relationship, Ana,' he said. 'I can't even open a letter from my dad, answer a text message from my sister or a phone call from my mother. I hurt the people I love every day, and there is no way I'm going to do that to you too. You deserve so much better than that.'

'I *know* I deserve more than that, Rhys. So does your family. So does our child.'

'I told you,' Rhys said, his eyes narrowing. 'I'm going to be a good dad—'

'Yet you know you can't be a good partner? A good brother? A good son? What's the difference, Rhys?'

'It *is* different. It has to be.'

Ana shook her head. 'I don't think it is, Rhys. I hope I'm wrong, but I don't think it is.'

She took a step out into the hallway, then

stopped, turned and walked right up to Rhys. Close enough that she had to tilt her chin up to meet his gaze.

'I want everything too, Rhys,' she said. 'I want everything with you—nothing less. But until you're willing to fight for everything— for me, for our child, for your family—I have to walk away.'

'You think if I just try harder I'll be normal again?' Rhys said sharply, incredulous. 'Fixed just like that?'

As if he could snap his fingers and the pieces of his broken life would all fit back together. As if he hadn't been fighting since the moment Jess died.

Ana's gaze was steady. 'You told me once that the right guy would fight for me. And you also told me that the next time I marry I should marry for love. That's good advice, Rhys, and *that's* what I deserve. What everyone deserves. Someone who will fight for love. For *my* love.'

She took a deep breath. In. Out.

'You need to work out a way to allow love into your life again, Rhys. It seems to me that you've been avoiding love for the past five years—to cope, I know, but that's no way to live your life. Our child is going to love you and, Rhys, I could so easily love you too—but I'm scared that you fear losing those you love so much you won't give love a chance in the first place. That you won't fight for it.' She paused. 'I think you need to get help, Rhys. I think—'

'I haven't had a panic attack in *years*, Ana,' Rhys said fiercely. 'I have it under control. But this is just who I am, okay? That's what I've been trying to tell you. It doesn't matter that I want *more*. I can't do it. I *can't*.'

Ana's gaze dropped. She walked to the door. She looked back and said firmly, 'I think you can, Rhys. Maybe not for me—I guess I'm not the woman you'll fight for.' Her voice cracked. 'But please, Rhys—fight for our baby.'

Then the door clicked shut behind her.

Rhys stood staring at the closed door of his suite for long, long minutes after Ana had gone.

'I could so easily love you too...'

'I guess I'm not the woman you'll fight for...'

'I think you need to get help...'

Ana's words swirled in his head, triggering visceral, conflicting, churning reactions: hope, frustration, anger.

She seemed to think it was so simple, when it was anything but. As if all he had to do was try harder—*fight* harder—and everything would be sorted. He'd be okay. They'd be okay.

And he was *nothing* like Ana's fiancé. The old Rhys wouldn't have waited around for his runaway bride to return, or let Ana walk away tonight. But he wasn't that guy any more. This wasn't about not caring enough, or not being the right guy. It was about realising that, no matter how right it *felt*, love just wasn't an option.

If he loved Ana and lost her...

He turned from the door, pacing the room.

It was done now. Over. There would be no more nights with Ana.

Even thinking those words was like a knife to his gut. But he needed to deal with that and move on. Focus on their child instead.

His gaze landed on the gift from Jas—the tiny baby outfit folded neatly on a side table. He picked the garments up, turning the fabric over and over in his hands.

He'd need to shop for baby supplies at some point. He'd need a cot and whatever else babies needed at his place as well as at Ana's. And clothes too. It would probably make sense to have sets of baby clothing at both homes.

That was the kind of conversation he needed

to have with Ana—about practical things, like where he should live in Vela Ada. They needed to talk about clothes and cots and baby baths—and more serious things, like working out custody arrangements, child support, access…

He realised he was gritting his teeth and felt his mind begin to race. Despite all this time, it was a familiar, instantly identifiable sensation.

No.

He dropped the baby clothes on the side table and sat on the edge of his bed. It had been so long since he'd allowed anxiety to shorten his breath, clutch at his throat and speed up his heart. Long enough that he'd gone beyond thinking he had it under control, and had actually begun to think it wasn't a part of him any more.

How naïve. How stupid he was.

He gripped his knees as he took long, deep breaths.

Stop, Rhys. Stop and think.

He told himself that once…twice.

He had a memory flash across his brain, of his doctor at the barracks walking him through this. *'You need to practise* before *you have your next attack, Rhys.'*

He'd thought it stupid. Humiliating, even.

Practising meant he was going to have more attacks. Accepting that. Accepting that reality. And he never had. Rhys North wasn't the kind of person, the kind of *man*, who had panic attacks.

Who practised them.

He'd never gone back. To that doctor, or to the barracks.

His brain spun in circles. Grasping at everything. At nothing. Memories, feelings, ideas. Fears...

Stop...stop...stop...stop...stop.

Stop. Stop and think.

Finally his thoughts began to slow and put themselves in order, into an arrangement he could manage that didn't threaten to overwhelm him.

Rhys opened his eyes—he had no idea at what point he'd squeezed them shut—then fell back onto the bed and deliberately relaxed his body, letting go of all his tension, from the tips of his fingers to his toes.

It was over.

'Your panic is induced by catastrophic thinking, Rhys.'

The memory of his doctor again.

'Your thinking patterns are the trigger. You need to learn to look at your fears more rationally, more realistically.'

But how was that possible? His wife had died without warning when he'd been helpless and on the other side of the world. In his career he'd seen the *worst* of humanity. He couldn't sugarcoat it. Terrible things *did* happen.

How could he pretend differently?

He'd asked his doctor that exact question, probably in far harsher language. His doctor's response had been something to do with a referral to a psychotherapist, about cognitive behavioural therapy...

He hadn't wanted to hear it. He didn't need some fancy psychotherapist to tell him to be more *realistic*. His life was as *real* as it got. As if pretending otherwise would make a difference.

So he'd managed it his own way.

Which had been working out just fine until he'd met Ana. Until he'd found out he was going to become a dad. Until he'd realised that hiding in the Dolomites had abruptly stopped being an option.

And until Ana had made him realise that, no matter how he cut it, he *had* abandoned his family, his friends…everyone who mattered to him.

And as he'd held those baby clothes in his hands, as he'd imagined Ana cradling their baby while he or she was dressed in suns and clouds, he'd imagined life without Ana. Without his child. Losing everything.

Losing everything again.

Losing all he *loved* again.

And as his brain had fallen into the abyss of what that might look like, what that might feel like, he'd lost himself in the panic he'd been avoiding for all these years. Not dealing with it, or processing it. But avoiding it.

He realised that for all he'd told Ana that his anxiety was under control, that he would be a great father, he'd actually had no place saying any of that if he really wasn't going to move from coping to living to *loving*…

Something needed to change.

He needed to fight.

Vela Ada's Christmas lights twinkled prettily as Ana was driven from the palace back to her home on the marina. It wasn't quite yet midnight—so still technically Christmas Day. She tried to focus on the lights—on admiring the angels, counting the number of reindeer... On filling her brain with anything but what had just happened. Anything but Rhys.

But, not surprisingly, it didn't work. By the time the driver slid the car to a stop at her front gate, only two facts whirled in her mind:

She had fallen in love with Rhys.

But Rhys didn't love her.

So much for getting out before she got hurt. So much for not making any more mistakes.

She'd been so *stupid* to sleep with him again. At the time it had felt like the most natural thing in the world, the most *right* thing in the world—but she'd just been kidding herself. She'd never stop wanting more, and getting out of his bed to leave had been one of the hardest things she'd ever done.

She should have just left. Not stopped and talked. What had *that* achieved other than underlining the fact that yet another man didn't want her? Didn't love her?

Rhys could dress it up by saying he wanted a relationship...but she didn't believe that. Rhys was prepared to find a way to be a good father, to overcome his grief and isolation and have a relationship with his child—and, oh, how desperately Ana prayed that he would deliver—but he wasn't prepared to do that for *her*.

He didn't love her. But she definitely loved him. And when had *that* happened? Maybe all the way back at the beginning, when he'd made her laugh in Castelrotto? Or when he'd told her mother at the airport that she was more than a princess? Or maybe simply every time he'd kissed her and the rest of the world had fallen away.

It was freezing in her courtyard, yet Ana still paused, hugging her coat around her as she stared at the fruit trees she'd decorated not much more than a week ago.

A week ago she'd refused any assistance from her guards and stood on a small stepladder as she'd wound Christmas lights around the branches of her orange tree, then her lemon tree. A week ago she hadn't known she was pregnant. She hadn't known she'd ever see Rhys again.

She hadn't known the pain of a broken heart.

The slam of a car door made Ana startle. She turned and watched as a familiar figure leapt up the few steps to her iron gate.

'Ana?' Rhys said, his gaze locking on hers.

Her guard Adrian glanced at her.

She shook her head. She'd learnt her lesson. She walked to her front door.

'Ana,' Rhys repeated, 'please.'

'*Doviđenja*, Rhys,' she said. *Goodbye, Rhys.*

She turned her back to him, fighting the tightness in her throat and the sting of her tears.

'No, Ana,' Rhys said. 'I'm not going anywhere.'

Her guard asked in Slavic if Ana would like Rhys removed.

She shook her head. 'No,' she said in English, 'he'll go now.'

'I won't,' Rhys said. 'I'm here to fight for you, Ana. I'm not just going to walk away.'

I'm here to fight for you.

Ana turned to face Rhys. Adrian was already at the gate, ready to move Rhys on—but Rhys only had eyes for her. The guard opened the gate, but before he could put a hand on Rhys— who had moved not one millimetre—Ana spoke.

'Adrian, leave us.'

The burly guard went still. 'You're sure, Your Highness?'

She wasn't—not at all. But even so she nodded.

Then suddenly it was only her and Rhys in the courtyard, the gate clanging shut behind him.

'I had a panic attack after you left,' Rhys said.

His blunt words hung in the frigid air between them.

'I'm a big guy, Ana,' he continued. 'I've always been taller and stronger than pretty much everyone else. My whole career was built on that strength—both physical and mental. It's who I am—who I *was*. But when Jess died, I crumbled. I was the opposite of strong. I lost my wife, I lost my future with her, and with the panic attacks I lost my identity.'

Ana's gaze traced the hard edges of Rhys's face.

'I needed to believe that I could overcome them myself. I needed to believe that I was in control, that I wasn't weak. That I was still strong. But of course I didn't deal with them at all. I just removed the trigger.' He swallowed. 'I removed love. By removing all the love in my life, I had nothing to fear losing.'

They'd moved closer together at some point, but Ana had no idea who had moved first.

'I knew I wanted more with you, Ana, but I told myself I wasn't capable of it—I was terrified that if I let myself love you I'd be weak again. But then you left, and I realised it was too late: I already love you.'

Ana swallowed, but it was too soon to know what his words meant.

'So I had a choice. I could run away to the mountains again, or I could stay and fight for you and for our baby. And then I realised it wasn't a choice at all. I want love in my life again. I *need* love in my life again. So I'm going to get help. I'm going to see the psychotherapist I should've seen all those years ago and learn how to be strong again.'

'I *never* thought you were weak, Rhys,' Ana said fiercely.

Rhys frowned, but Ana continued before he could argue.

'Grief is not a weakness, Rhys. It's a part of life. I'm so sorry it's played such a big part in yours, but it's never made you weak. You're *strong*, Rhys. You didn't even know me and you supported me when I turned up on your mountain. Then you followed me to Vela Ada to be by my side when I needed your strength. You've been by my side every step of this crazy, unexpected journey we've taken together and you've made me stronger.'

'You make me stronger too, Ana,' Rhys said, his voice rough with emotion. 'I—'

But then he stopped and suddenly looked upwards.

So did Ana, and as she did something touched her cheek.

Snow.

'It's *snowing*,' Ana breathed in wonder.

Suddenly it was impossible not to touch Rhys, and he must have thought the same about her as his arms were around her and he'd dragged her close.

'My first white Christmas,' Ana said softly.

'*Our* first Christmas,' Rhys said. 'I hope there are many, many more to come. With you and with our baby.'

'There will be,' Ana said, standing on tiptoes, a breath away from kissing him. 'I love you, Mr North.'

Then he kissed her, beneath the fairy lights and the flakes of snow.

When they eventually came up for air, Rhys's words were hot against her cheek.

'I love you too, Your Highness.'

* * * * *

LET'S TALK
Romance

For exclusive extracts, competitions
and special offers, find us online:

f facebook.com/millsandboon

◎ @millsandboonuk

🐦 @millsandboon

Or get in touch on 0844 844 1351*

For all the latest titles coming soon,
visit millsandboon.co.uk/nextmonth

*Calls cost 7p per minute plus your phone company's price per
minute access charge